THE STREET OF
BUTTERFLIES

We gratefully acknowledge the support of the Canada Council for the Arts and the Ontario Arts Council for our publishing program. We also acknowledge the financial support of the Government of Canada.

Cover design: Val Fullard

The Street of Butterflies is a work of fiction. All the characters and situations portrayed in this book are fictitious and any resemblance to persons living or dead is purely coincidental.

Library and Archives Canada Cataloguing in Publication

Yalfani, Mehri, author
    The street of butterflies / short fiction by Mehri Yalfani.

(Inanna poetry & fiction series)
Issued in print and electronic formats.
ISBN 978-1-77133-425-9 (softcover).--ISBN 978-1-77133-426-6 (epub).--
ISBN 978-1-77133-427-3 (Kindle).--ISBN 978-1-77133-428-0 (pdf)

    I. Title. II. Series: Inanna poetry and fiction series

PS8597.A47S77 2017   C813'.54   C2017-905369-8
                                              C2017-905370-1

Printed and bound in Canada

Inanna Publications and Education Inc.
210 Founders College, York University
4700 Keele Street, Toronto, Ontario M3J 1P3 Canada
Telephone: (416) 736-5356   Fax (416) 736-5765
Email: inanna.publications@inanna.ca Website: www.inanna.ca

THE STREET OF BUTTERFLIES

stories by

MEHRI YALFANI

inanna poetry & fiction series

INANNA PUBLICATIONS AND EDUCATION INC.
TORONTO, CANADA

For my family

Table of Contents

—ᴍ—

Books

—⟋⟋⟋—

For my brother, Mohsen Yalfani, a playwright, who spent four years in prison during the time of the Shah. Though he was freed by the revolution, he was persecuted after the Islamic Republic became the absolute power in Iran and thus forced to flee the country.

NOZAR OPENED THE DOOR of the house and peeked into the alley. The streetlights were off but the lights were on in some of the houses and their front yards, though they barely lit the alley. For a few months now, there hadn't been any air attacks, so some of the neighbours no longer worried about the war between Iran and Iraq in Khuzestan, almost one thousand kilometres from Tehran.

Nozar was breathing hard from lugging five large garbage bags full of books down the front stairs. He had made three trips. The car had been parked only a few metres away from the front door. Nevertheless, he had started the engine, put the car in reverse, and then eased it as close as possible to the entrance. Very quietly, he placed the bags one by one inside the trunk.

Sara was sitting on the bottom step, watching Nozar's ordeal each time he came down. She was wearing a loose cotton dress with short sleeves, and was very still and silent. With her hair tied back, her sunken eyes seemed even bigger. Her frightened expression was an extra burden on Nozar, who was preoccupied

1

by what he was doing. With a few days' growth of whiskers, his complexion looked darker and he appeared older; his tall, sturdy body was wet with sweat and hunched slightly. He looked at Sara, sitting mutely on the stairs, watching him, her eyes filled with desperation. He softened his voice and said, "You'd better go upstairs and rest. You need…"

The motor of a passing car interrupted him. Nozar listened carefully until the thrum of the motor faded away. With the same calm, soothing tone he continued, "I'll finish the job in an hour and then I'll come right back. I promise." He continued ferociously, "These wicked books! We have to get rid of them. They are the reason for our…"

This time it was the sound of faraway shooting that made him stop abruptly.

Sara couldn't bring herself to say a word. She smiled anxiously and this made Nozar even more nervous, the silence between them, and blanketing the neighbourhood, a heavy fog pressing around them.

The books sitting in Nozar's trunk were dear to Sara. She had spent money and time on them, enjoyed reading them, and had learned from them. She was proud of having them, considered them valuable assets, like she would a dear friend. They were something that she could count on, that gave her pleasure, joy, happiness, and they had filled the dreary days and nights when Nozar was in prison. They were her prestige, her dignity, an integral part of her life. She had shared them with Nozar, her friends, and even with people she didn't know well, but who had read the same books—the very same books she was now going to throw away, disappearing them from her life.

Sara was quiet. It seemed to her that a film was playing in front of her, and everything seemed unreal.

From the bottom step, she could see only a small part of the alley. Nozar closed the trunk of the car quietly and walked toward her. She stood up, her hands in her pockets, let Nozar hug her, kiss her forehead and lips, but she was remote. He cupped her face with his hands, looked at her in the eyes, and said, "Don't worry. Many people are doing the same. Everybody is throwing away the books that might cause them problems. Farahzad's and Varamin's ditches, and even those of Shahre Ray and the roads out of Tehran, are all full of books people have thrown away. I won't go very far. So, I'll be back soon."

"I'd better come with you," Sara said, releasing herself from Nozar's arms with a sudden jerk. She looked at her dress and continued, "I'll change in a minute, wear my black chador, and accompany you. With me, it will look less suspicious."

"Don't even think about it," Nozar said firmly. Sara had already started climbing the steps toward the second floor. Nozar held her arm gently and continued, "Nothing will happen. I promise."

Sara did not resist. She breathed deeply, as if she wanted to release a burden from her chest, and said, "You're right. Many people have done the same. Last night Bahram and Kami took a few garbage bags of books out and threw them into Far-ahzad's ditches. They said there were thousands of books in the highway ditches and even in some other areas right in the city. Those books might have belonged to people who didn't have a car to drive further out of the city. You see…" A lump in her throat and tears in her eyes prevented her from saying more.

"You see," repeated Nozar confidently, but she could read the unspoken words in his eyes. He nodded sympathetically, "I know that you are sorry to lose the books. I feel the same, but we have no choice except to get rid of them."

Sara smothered her tears with a forced smile as Nozar ac-companied her up the rest of the stairs to their apartment. He hugged her tightly and kissed her again, this time avoiding her eyes. "Stay calm and rest," he said. Then he separated himself from Sara and looked at his watch; it was ten past eleven. He said goodbye, climbed back down the stairs, and closed the door quietly behind him. Sara listened to the sound of the engine starting, then flew down the stairs, out the door, and rushed to the driver's window. Nozar hit the brakes suddenly, then lowered the window and said, "Please go inside and try to relax. I'll be back in an hour." He pressed on the gas and the car jerked forward.

Sara climbed up the stairs again slowly, feeling cold in her hands and feet and went back inside the house. She stood at the top until the sound of the car faded away and silence dominated again.

The apartment felt empty, as if a group of noisy friends had suddenly left a few minutes earlier. The bare bookshelves were ugly wounds, hurting her. She sat on the sofa and quietly sobbed, tears streaming down her cheeks. She didn't try to wipe them away. She laughed in the middle of her crying, told herself she was "crazy," then calmed herself down, repeating Nozar's words out loud: "Nothing will happen." She went to the bedroom to look for something to busy herself with, but she couldn't find anything that could occupy her. Sluggishly, she made her way back to the living room, sat on the sofa and turned the TV on, but there was no programming. The only sound in the room was the steady *tick tock* of the clock. She jumped at the sound of another shooting, also far away. Her heart was racing. "No, nothing will happen," she repeated to herself.

She wished she could phone a friend or her sister but it was too late. She went to the kitchen to wash the dishes but Nozar had already done them. Restless, she returned to the living room and picked up the book that was on coffee table—one of the few remaining deemed acceptable to own—a novel. She opened it to the page she had bookmarked, read half a page, but lost her concentration and put it back on the table. She drifted to the bedroom, found her basket of knitting, and carried it into the living room. She sat on the sofa again and rifled through the different colours and textures of yarn. Finally, she chose white and pink. She listened to the silence and wondered listlessly about what to knit, decided finally to start working on a sweater for her baby. Her hands moved automatically and rhythmically. For a while she was absorbed by her hands shaping the yarn, but suddenly she lost the rhythm and stopped. The shriek of an ambulance's siren crossing a nearby street startled her momentarily, but then the ticking of the clock was once again the only noise in the living room. Sara carefully examined what she had knitted. It was too small to be a sweater, even for newborn baby. She undid her work and abandoned the knitting needles and yarn on the sofa.

When she heard the voices of two men talking in the alley, she hurriedly made her way to the kitchen. She stood by the window and peered out without turning the light on, but the men were gone, the sound of their distant footsteps the only sign they had been there. Darkness didn't allow much of the alley to be visible; there was only a dim light, perhaps from the stars or the crescent moon. She could barely see the houses on the other side. The nearest house, which belonged to Mr. Imani, was in total darkness. She imagined the whole fami-ly—Mr. Imani, Mrs. Fariba, and their two little daughters—in their sweet sleep, far from the agonies. Their Mercedes was parked under a trellis covered in vines close to the gate. There were stars in the sky but not like the stars in Kerman's sky on a moonless night, which to Sara had always looked like a dark carpet woven with diamonds. *If I weren't pregnant,* she thought, *we could go to Kerman and stay there with my parents for a few weeks.*

The tree by the alley was also invisible in darkness, but a whispering breeze caressed Sara's arms and neck. She returned to the living room. It was almost midnight. There was more shooting and the siren of another distant ambulance. Coldness penetrated her bones and she shivered. *Driving to Farahzad and returning to Amirabad should take about an hour,* she thought. *At any moment Nozar's car will enter the alley and stop under the kitchen window. There it is....* The sound of a car brought a small smile to her face and her heart started to beat faster. But the car didn't stop and a chilly shiver replaced her momentary joy. Midnight's silence was getting heavier. She went to the bedroom and came back with a blanket. She wrapped herself in it and huddled on the sofa. She tried to rest but a sudden cramp gripped the muscles under her belly. The clock on the wall moved ahead and midnight passed. The sound of another car in the alley made her jump, but it stopped before reaching her house. She heard the car door slam shut and even though she had lost hope, she didn't want to give up completely. She went into the kitchen once again peer at the alley from the window, but a new pain in her belly forced her to sit down at the table.

She wasn't aware when the clock's hands passed one. She remained sitting at the table, her mind a blank. There was no sound in the alley, and if a car passed occasionally, she didn't get up to look out the window. The thought that Nozar might not come back paralyzed her. She stopped thinking about tomorrow and about what might have happened to Nozar. Instead, the past captured her mind and she was taken back to eight years ago.

Five months after Nozar's confinement in Evin prison, she went to visit him. He was being kept in a cage with walls of glass, as if he was a dangerous beast. He had lost weight and most of his legs were covered in bandages, but Sara was happy to see him alive. After his sentencing—ten years in prison—he was allowed weekly visits. He gradually gained more strength, and encouraged Sara to be strong, too. Later, Sara tried not to show weakness behind the thick glass that separated them in the meeting room, their voices buffered by the commotion coming from the crowds of people visiting other inmates. He had asked her to bring him some books and she was pleased that he would be able to use his time in prison to enrich his knowledge.

Five years passed and the murmur of revolution and free-dom filled the streets and hearts of the people. They had lived together for only four months before Nozar was arrested and imprisoned. The promise of their reunion, along with the excitement of the coming revolution, was a sweet dream.

When he was released from the prison and they were together again, all they wanted was to relive all those years and days, all the moments that had been stolen from them during the five years they had been separated by a brutal force.

A few months after Nozar's release, Sara found out she was pregnant, and she wondered what to do. They discussed the possibility of an abortion. Nozar left the decision to Sara. Fascinated by an unknown creature growing inside her, she delayed making a decision. But when she considered the baby's need for lifelong commitment, she was reluctant to have it. She wanted to have her whole life for herself. The years she had waited for Nozar's freedom—the years that had passed between the time she was twenty-four and twenty-nine—had been stolen from her, and now she had a thirst for life. This baby wouldn't let her be free, wouldn't let her live as she liked. When she had some bleeding in the second month of her pregnancy, she had thought it might be a sign that she should have an abortion, but then something prevented her from doing it—a feeling that the child represented a deeper tie between Nozar and herself; a physical bond, perhaps. The child would be the continuation of her life, and his, after they both ceased to exist. These thoughts encouraged her to keep the baby and suddenly she allowed herself to be thrilled by the creature growing inside her body. She finally announced her decision to Nozar: "The baby will be born."

Crumpled on the sofa, lost in her thoughts, when the clock clicked at three a.m., she was startled. It seemed every object in the apartment was asking her, "What happened to Nozar? Why is he late? Where is he?"

Sara was certain that Nozar would not come back. She was certain when she had watched him place the bags of books inside the trunk of the car, certain when he had hugged her, when he had looked in her eyes and said, "I'll be back quickly. It won't take more than an hour. Don't worry. You rest and relax." Sara had listened to him without saying anything, but her certainty about him not coming back had filled her with dread, had made her feet and hands ice cold. Nozar had hugged her warmly again, then murmured against her cheek, "Don't worry. No need for you to come. You shouldn't be anxious."

Cars passed infrequently and nothing disturbed the deep silence that filled her apartment and the entire neighbourhood.

Sara lay down again on the sofa. She was certain about tomorrow too—the revolutionary guards would come and take her as well, and then.... She couldn't imagine what might happen afterward. Instead, the past rushed back to her and filled her thoughts once again. She knew the past would be repeated. Nozar was imprisoned the first time because of his book of poetry, a best seller.

He had been captured on the street and that night the Savakies had invaded their home. She had opened the door and they had rushed in like a victorious army conquering an enemy castle. Their apartment didn't have much furniture; it wasn't yet a real place to live. They only had a small bed in the bedroom; a sofa, the same one that she was lying on now, a desk; and a rug that her father had given them as a marriage gift. Their books were still in boxes or on the floor. Their pots and pans and dishes were barely a handful.

All those moments returned to her. It was the middle of night when the Savakies banged on the door and rang the bell insistently. She had raced to the door, imagining it was Nozar and that she would fall into his arms. Instead, she faced five men with cold faces who warned her to cooperate, otherwise she would face dire consequences. They destroyed the house: ripped the mattress, the pillows, broke the bed, pulled everything out the kitchen cabinets and knocked holes in the walls with their fists to be sure nothing was hidden there. Sara sat on the sofa immobile and watched them—it was a nightmare. They collected every book they considered a crime to own: novels, short stories, even science books. They didn't tell her where they had taken Nozar.

Now Sara was certain they would come again to search the house and this time take her, too. She abandoned herself to this destiny.

The sound of a truck bringing milk for Rastgoo Supermarket woke her up. In the June sunshine she could see the outline of other houses on the street and the maple tree in the yard, whose branches reached the window. Cars passed in the street, but the apartment was quiet. Even though she was certain that Nozar would not be back, she could not quell the flutter of hope inside her. Under her skin, she still felt cold, and so she again wrapped herself in a blanket. She didn't have the strength to get up and go to her bedroom, mesmerized as she was by the sound of the traffic close by and further away. Sara felt another cramp move through her belly muscles, reminding her of the baby growing inside. She remembered something her mother had said: "You will feel the baby's first movement as a shivering of your belly muscles." Sara smiled faintly, and thought she would tell Nozar that the she had felt the baby move as soon as he got home.

Sunshine lit the living room suddenly, as if warning Sara this day would be different from other days. She got up, collected a few necessary things in a small bag, changed from her nightgown into a light summer dress, pulled on a black chador over her head, and then climbed down the stairs hurriedly. She was partway down when she heard the distinct sound of a car parking by the door. She stopped, held her breath, and waited. Time stood still. For a moment, the silence was deafening. She strained to listen. Would she hear the sound of a key turning in the lock, of the door opening, and see Nozar appear on the threshold with his happy, warm smile? Or would the doorbell ring loudly and insistently, as it had eight years before?

American Chocolate

—ᗰ—

WHEN I WAS IN GRADE TEN I had the worst New Year's holiday I'd ever had. The first day of the school holiday was fine. I spent it with my immediate family, along with my aunts, uncles, cousins, and other close relatives. We had gathered at my grandparents' house, as was the custom, to honour my grandparents, the oldest and most dignified members of the clan. But my two younger brothers got sick that day and after that, for the rest of the holiday, I had to stay home to look after them.

The Iranian New Year is celebrated on March 21, which coincides with the first day of spring, so we were observing the revival of nature as well. It was unfortunate that I had to spend the holiday confined indoors with two sick brothers. I should have spent the time outside, enjoying nature, and playing with my friends.

Hamadan, the city where I was born and raised, is in the west of Iran, at the foot of the Alvand Mountains. Hamadan, historically, is reputed to be the first capital of Persia, the ancient name for Iran. The only remainder of Hamadan's magnificent history is a stone lion that sits in a deserted area far from the centre of the city. Before the Arabs invaded Persia and destroyed all its glories, the stone lion had been located atop the city's gate. It is said that the stone lion has the power to make wishes come true. I always felt pity for the poor stone lion, forced to witness the desperation of people for whom God did nothing.

But during the holiday, I often thought about going to the lion and wishing for freedom from my sick brothers!

Finally, the two-week school holiday was over. When it was time to return to school, I was like a bird who'd found a way to fly out of its cage.

To get to my school, I had to walk along Booali Street and past the monument of Ebne Sina, a famous physician and scientist-philosopher from one thousand years ago. The monument is a symbol of pride for our city. The peak of a tall and magnificent minaret that stands next to the monument seems to touch the blue sky. These were a soothing contrast to my dreary New Year's holiday spent inside, catering to the demands of my brothers.

When I entered the schoolyard, I saw my friend Mina, a classmate since grade one. She ran over, hugged me, and handed me a parcel: "It's for you." Mina began pouring out the story of her trip to Tehran, the capital of our country—a place I dream of visiting once in a while. I opened the parcel. It was a tiny, silver bird hanging on thin chain. I'd never had anything like it before and thanked her profusely.

The first class was history. As our teacher lectured us in his coarse, husky voice, the door to the classroom opened and our janitor popped her head in. The teacher stopped talking, angry at this unusual intrusion. The class sat immobile; we were in a state of suspense and fear.

Ignoring the teacher's irritation, the janitor scanned the class, obviously looking for someone. Surprisingly, her eyes landed on me and she told me that I had to go to the office. In that moment, I thought my heart was going to stop beating.

Being called to the office usually signaled a death in the family, an accident, some kind of bad behaviour, or a very bad report card. For the grade ten students who were eligible to marry, it sometimes meant a suitor, a very impatient one, unable to wait for a few hours to see his presumptive bride when she got home from school. All these possibilities crossed my mind as I followed the janitor to the office, my heart hammering in my chest. Even when I noticed the exhilaration on the face of the vice-principal, I never imagined there might be extraordinary news for me, news that could change my whole life as abruptly as the wind takes a feather to the sky.

The vice-principal gently placed her hand on my back and led me to a chair. Assertive and open-minded, she was a strong believer in women's education and liberation. Whenever she had the chance, she advised us not to yield to our parents' will to marry before finishing our education and instead to get a degree or a job that would allow us to be independent.

The vice-principal's voice, like a glass of cool water, calmed my racing heart. She was wearing a navy jacket over a sky-blue shirt and a pale grey skirt. I could smell a trace of delicate lilac perfume. Sitting in front of me, she looked like a movie star.

"My dear girl," she said, "you have been chosen from among all the grade ten students in Hamadan to go to Beirut to study at the American University. Your marks and your behaviour have been remarkable over the past few years. The principal, your teachers, and I, believe that you are the best candidate for this scholarship. We know that you wish to continue your studies and pursue an education in medicine at the University of Tehran, so we referred you to the committee and they have selected you."

Before I could digest what I was hearing, she continued, "These opportunities are part of the American plan to educate the citizens of the Third World countries, and improve their quality of life."

I had heard the term "Third World countries" from American visitors to our school. They usually came in pairs, a man and a woman, or two women, and often showed us a short film about American lives, American children, and American plans for the underdeveloped countries.

Frankly, the term offended me. I didn't like to hear it from the vice-principal, who had taught us to be proud of our nationality. Deep in my heart, I couldn't believe that Persia, with its glorious past—one of the oldest monarchies in the world before the Islam invasion, a land with more than three thousand years of history—would be considered a "Third World country."

The vice-principal's words left me speechless for another reason. Since grade seven, when I started to read novels and poetry, I had been captivated by literature, and one of my dreams was to become a famous writer. Study medicine? I'd never expressed that intention to anyone, although it was my family's wish for me. Even so, I knew that being invited to attend the American University was an opportunity beyond my wildest dreams. Going to Beirut was like a gate opening into heaven.

I jumped in my chair when the bell rang for recess, still not quite trusting what I'd heard. The vice-principal repeated her words even more fervently, and congratulated me again on my bright future. Then she pointed to a box of chocolates on her desk, and invited me to take one. "It's American chocolate," she smiled. "They brought it for the school to celebrate your achievement." I took one and put it in my mouth, startled by its pungent flavour. I left the office with the bittersweet taste of chocolate filling my mouth.

Mina and some other students had gathered by the office door to wait for me. They encircled me, asking excitedly what was going on. I couldn't answer them; I was still stunned by the news. Was it true? Was I really going to go to Beirut, a city described as the "Paris of the Middle East" on the shore of the Mediterranean Sea?

Mina pulled me aside, sympathy in her eyes. "What happened? Tell me," she asked.

"I don't know," I said, swallowing the last of chocolate. Its acrid taste was still bothering me.

"What do you mean, you don't know? Are you going to get married?"

"No," I said, offended.

"What is it then?"

The other students gathered around us. My eyes met those of Pooran. She was standing a little apart, as if she didn't care what might have happened to me. She was a self-important girl from a wealthy family who competed with me in many subjects. But her marks were never as high as mine. She was tall and slender, with long braids falling down her back. I looked at her directly. "They're going to send me to Beirut."

The students crowded around me more closely, their eyes full of surprise and envy. "Beirut? For what purpose?"

"To study medicine," I said loudly, to be sure Pooran would hear.

Returning to the classroom, I felt weightless. Happiness engulfed me like a thick cloud. The vice-principal's words had finally sunk in. I passed the rest of the day in a state of ecstasy. My classmates stared at me as if I possessed a special nobility. I smiled at them, grateful to my lucky star.

The news lit the gloomy atmosphere at home with hope and pride. My fear that my parents would be against the idea vanished as soon as they realized the scholarship would bring me prosperity. That their young daughter might study at an American university was beyond their imagining, and the fact that I had been offered such a golden opportunity transformed me into their genius child. From then on, whenever we heard a plane crossing the sky, my little sister called me, imagining that the plane had come to take me to Beirut.

For the next two months, I was the centre of attention at home and at school. There wasn't a single day when my friends didn't talk about my good fortune. My older brother had given me a pamphlet about the American University that featured photographs of smiling girls and boys with piles of books under their arms. Their happy faces populated my fantasies.

Two weeks before final exams, again, during history class, the janitor appeared at the classroom door and asked me to go to the office. Waiting there were two strangers, Americans. I was mesmerized by the man's big body, his bulging blue eyes, and his nearly bald head. The woman, tall and slim, fixed her inquisitive black eyes on me as I spoke. They questioned me about my family, and I did my best in my broken English to answer. But when I told them about my father's job—an accountant in a construction company—and his income, they seemed to lose interest in me. I was perplexed. After the bell rang for recess, my classmates gathered around me, wanting to know what had happened. Pooran was among them, staring at me with her large, dark eyes, her braids curled on the top of her head, fixed with a shiny green barrette. Then the janitor came out into the yard and this time called Pooran to the office. Afterward, she didn't say a single word to anyone about her summons, but I worried that the Americans' might prefer to give the scholarship to her. Pooran's father owned a large pharmacy in the main square of the city. Her family had been wealthy for generations, and their roots were spread all over Hamadan.

It seemed obvious to me then that Pooran was the preferable candidate for the American university, not me. But I couldn't easily abandon the dream of going to Beirut. One day I went to the barren area where the stone lion lay down on the ground, looking lonely and miserable in the late spring afternoon sunshine. I put my hands on the stone and cried desperately, beseeching the lion to make my wish come true.

I waited until the very last day of school, although I was burning to my bone to know what had happened to my scholarship. Finally, I went to the office and knocked on the door. The vice-principal opened the door and came out into the hall. She was wearing a flowery dress with short sleeves. Her face looked tired and her hair was a little dishevelled. Her lipstick had faded.

She put her hands on my shoulders, and began, "My dear girl...."

She didn't need to continue. Her sympathetic eyes and pitying voice clearly communicated her news. I had not been chosen by the Americans. She and the principal had done their best to convince them that I was more intelligent than Pooran, but they had not been successful. The vice-principal encouraged me not to give up hope, to study as hard as I always had. I would stand highest in my entrance exam for the medical faculty at the University of Tehran, she predicted, and I wouldn't need to go far away to a foreign country or beg Americans for assistance. After almost fifteen minutes, I came to my senses and thanked her for her words. Her hands were still on my shoulders, and her compassion touched me. "Don't worry. You're young and there will be many opportunities in front of you." She wished me a relaxing summer and suggested I forget about the American university.

I said goodbye with a lump in my throat, then rushed to the washroom to hide my tears of humiliation from Mina and the others. I came out only when I was sure no one was in the schoolyard and walked straight home. I chose to go the long way, through the alleys, not along Booali Street and past the monument of Ebne Sina. I didn't want him to observe my tears either.

A few weeks later, as I sat on our veranda having tea with my aunt, my mother, my younger brothers, and my sister, a plane appeared in the blue sky. A sharp pain in my chest brought tears to my eyes. Everyone in my family had been careful not mention the scholarship. But my sister was too young to realize what had happened. She pointed to the plane and said, "Look, it's coming to take Mehri to Beirut." My mother slapped my sister's hand, told her not to say that ever again. My sister started to cry. By then, my own tears had already taken shape and were streaming down my face.

The following fall, when I started grade eleven, I was astonished to see Pooran in the yard, talking to Mina. I hugged Mina and then reluctantly hugged Pooran, too. I was wondering whether to ask her about scholarship, but then, I couldn't stand it anymore and blurted out, "Why are you here? What happened to the scholarship?"

"My father wouldn't let me accept it."

"Why?" I asked, stupefied.

"Because it was rightfully yours and...."

I didn't hear the rest of her words. I hugged her again and we walked into the classroom together.

Inexplicable

—⟋⟋⟍—

ZINAT WAS SITTING ON THE SOFA, watching television, and Taher, as usual, had taken refuge in his own room after having had a light dinner. Zinat didn't remember how long it had been since they had started sleeping in separate bedrooms. It might have begun when they moved to this apartment and she got into the habit of staying up late at night. When Taher would ask her, "Don't you want to go to bed?" Zinat would say no timidly and without looking at him, as if going to bed with her husband was a sin. She never told him she was waiting for Mahan, but Taher could see in her eyes that she hadn't lost hope that Mahan would come home, and that maybe he would arrive late at night. He would shake his head without saying a word, pick up the newspaper, go to what used to be their bedroom, and quietly close the door. Then there would just be Zinat and the TV. She would turn the volume low so as not to disturb Taher and as she watched the images on the screen, her thoughts would wander. Sometimes she would fall asleep on the sofa without turning the TV off. Then she would wake up startled, turn her head to look at the apartment door, waiting for Mahan to open it and come in. After a while, she succumbed to a deep depression, sighing helplessly and muttering to herself that he wouldn't show up that night, either. She would turn the TV off, go to Mahan's room, spread a sheet over his bed and lie down, covering herself with a blanket and falling into a deep asleep.

Waiting for Mahan, her thoughts often went back to when they were living in their previous house. Their bedrooms were on the second floor. The room she had shared with Taher, and Mahan's room, faced the front yard, but Parastoo's room looked out on their backyard and the neighbours' house.

Parastoo bedroom's walls had been covered with posters of actors, actresses, and singers. Zinat remembered one of them very clearly, though she'd forgotten his name. Parastoo said he was a black man, but in the poster he looked like a white woman with long black hair.

Mahan's bedroom had two big posters: Chegoara, on the back of his bedroom door, and the other one, a tall black man aiming a ball at a basketball hoop; it looked as if a strong wind had lifted him up, his arm and shoulder muscles bulging as he holds and aims the ball. Zinat was familiar with Chegoara's name, as she'd heard it often and had seen his photograph everywhere. There was also a book in Mahan's room about him, with the same photo on its cover.

During those times, Parastoo was busy with a bunch of girlfriends coming and going. When she finished high school, she took the university exam but failed. Then she fell in love with the neighbours' son. They married, and during the war between Iran and Iraq, they left Iran for Germany to continue their education. They finished school, but preferred to live in Germany; they came back to Iran only for brief visits.

Mahan was a university student in those days and was hardly ever at home, even though the universities were closed. Mahan disappeared a few months after Parastoo's departure for Germany. He had left the house one day as he did every day. He never told Zinat or Taher where he was going, but he always came back, sometimes late at night, sometimes early the next morning.

Zinat had forgotten the actual date that Mahan had left the house for the last time, but he had called home a few days later. Zinat had gone shopping, so when he phoned Taher had answered the ring. When Zinat returned, Taher told her that Mahan had called and said that he'd be back within a few days.

Zinat didn't know how many months and years had passed since that call, and Mahan hadn't come back. Whenever she asked about Mahan, Taher shook his head and muttered sarcastically, "You're talking nonsense." If it was late at night, he barely answered her at all, and simply announced he was going to bed.

When they were living in their house, Zinat had had more space for herself. She was always busy in the kitchen cooking, or in the front yard caring for the garden, or cleaning Mahan's or Parastoo's bedroom. She could talk to Mahan as much as she wanted and Taher couldn't hear her, and ask, "Who are you talking to?" When he did, she would look at him and say nothing.

Parastoo came back from Germany to visit after a few years. She stayed with them for a while, encouraged them to sell the house and buy an apartment, which she thought would be more comfortable for them, as they were getting old and fragile. Zinat felt the apartment was too small, with the bedrooms, living room, kitchen and bathroom all on the same floor. It had a small balcony, though, and Zinat liked to sit on the balcony and watch the street, always full of noise and traffic, especially in the afternoon, when the children came back from school with their backpacks slung over their shoulders. The girls in their uniforms and head scarves looked like a flock of birds, chirping and moving in unison. She remembered when Parastoo and Mahan were younger and attended the same school. In those days, Parastoo didn't have to wear a head scarf. Sometimes, she spotted a little boy who looked like her own Mahan. She fell into a deep melancholy, and when she regained herself, Taher was at the balcony door calling her inside. Night had fallen, so the lights were on and Taher had arranged the table for supper. They ate for the most part in silence, sometimes exchanging only a few words.

The apartment was jammed with furniture and a few potted plants. The plants reminded her of her house and her front yard with its two small gardens. She loved her gardens, especially the geraniums and petunias that would flower abundantly in summer. She used to like to wake up early in the morning and go out to the front yard where she would sit on a bench and watch the sky as it slowly turned a deep blue. The gardens were verdant, full of different kinds of flowers, and the sparrows would fly joyfully among the tree branches. The green gate at the end of courtyard was covered by a vine that stretched up to the top of the trellis, making shade for the car that was parked underneath. The car had gone along with the house.

She remembered the hours she spent in that house staring at the front door, waiting for it to open. Mahan would enter and she would run toward him, hug him tightly, and ask, "Where have you been, my dear boy? Why are you so late? You said you'd be back soon."

The sun would not have yet reached her feet when Taher would call her. Inside, Taher would have arranged the table for the breakfast with cheese, bread, jam and butter. The samovar was boiling with a teapot on the top of it. Taher, who had already had his own breakfast, sat on a folded blanket, leaning on a cushion and reading a newspaper. He would look at Zinat with an inexplicable question in his eyes, and this disturbed her. If he asked her what she did in the yard, she would look back at him bewildered. Sometimes, she blurted out that she was waiting for Mahan. Then Taher would shake his head, disappointed, and say nothing. But there was something in his silence that bothered Zinat. She wished everyone would simply leave her alone so that she would be able to wait for Mahan as long as she wanted. She had lost interest in cleaning the house, cooking, or tidying up—all she could do was stare at the door, imagine it being opened and Mahan coming in. Even though she knew that the door bell was broken, once in a while she went to the door to see who was there, and if

Taher asked her why, she would be cross at him and grumble, "Didn't you hear the door bell? I heard the bell ringing." When there was no one there, she would mumble something, accuse the children in the alley playing soccer. Taher had told her a hundred times, even a thousand times, that Mahan had a key. "He always used his key to open the door. Have you forgotten?" No, she hadn't forgotten, but, well, she thought he might have left his key at home or he might have lost it. After so many years...

When they moved to the apartment, Zinat collected all Mahan's books and put them in boxes. She took the posters off the walls, rolled them up carefully, and placed them on top of the books, planning to eventually hang them up again in his new bedroom. But when they moved to the new apartment she couldn't find the posters or even the boxes of books. She took a few photos from her album and gave them to a shop close to their new place and had them enlarged. She framed the photos, and hung them on Mahan's empty bedroom walls. The photos filled Mahan's room as if Mahan himself was there.

Afterward, Zinat looked at the photos, a smile on her face, and said, "You know that I love you so much. Why don't you come back, my dear? I miss you so much." She chatted to Mahan's photos for a while almost daily. When she was in the living room, she talked to the images on the television. When she was alone at home, she talked to her son as long as she liked, but when Taher was around, he usually heard her and would come out from his bedroom, puzzled, and ask, "Were you talking on the phone?" Zinat would look at him as if she'd done something wrong. Taher didn't show any anger, just muttered, "I thought you were talking on the phone." Zinat smiled as if she was saying, you know everything, don't you?

It was almost dawn when the key turned in the lock. Zinat was sure that it was Mahan. Her heart started pounding, its echo in her ears as loud as a big drum. She thought she should go to Taher's room and wake him up. Was it possible that Taher was asleep and wouldn't hear that Mahan was home? But all her strength had been drained from her body and her legs were so weak, she couldn't bring herself to stand up. Mahan walked toward her and she reached out for him, her voice faltering, "Mahan."

She couldn't believe this man was her own Mahan. He was vaguely familiar, but he was also reserved and formal towards her, like a stranger.

When Mahan left them, they still lived in the two-storey house. He had the key for that house, not this apartment where they'd moved years after he had disappeared. How did he get the key to this apartment? Zinat couldn't figure that out. Probably Parastoo had given it to him, she guessed. Zinat stared at Mahan, her eyes searching his features. Mahan tried to bring Zinat back to herself and said, "Mother, why haven't you gone to bed? It's almost dawn."

Zinat coloured crimson. Sweat beaded on her forehead and on her upper lip, and her body flushed. She wanted to say, "Where have you been all these many years, my son?" But her mouth was dry and her tongue was like a piece of wood—the words did not take shape. She sank into her own disturbed thoughts, but Mahan's voice brought her back, and this time she was sure that this man was her own Mahan.

Mahan said, "Your apartment looks like a cage…" He didn't continue. She had heard the same thing come from Taher. When Parastoo chose this apartment for them and encouraged them to buy it, Taher had carefully inspected it and it was then he had said the place looked like a cage. But Zinat hadn't said anything. She didn't want to hurt Parastoo, who had come a long way after so many years to arrange a nice, comfortable place for her parents. She just let her eyes wander randomly around the place and said quietly, "Well, it's only a flat, that's it." She opened the door to the balcony and the roar of buses and trucks rushed in.

She asked Mahan, "Why are you so late?" And then continued hesitantly, "You're older."

Mahan stared at Zinat, and the look in his eyes bewildered her. It was always the same; she panicked when people looked straight into her eyes and she herself could not see what was in their eyes.

But now that Mahan had finally returned, she should be happy again. But this Mahan didn't look like her own Mahan. He mostly looked like Taher, who hadn't wakened to see how Mahan had aged. She wanted to yell, "Look? Our Mahan's back! Didn't I tell you he'd be back? I always told you he would come back. But you...."

Taher never believed her. He never told her directly that he didn't believe her, but the way he looked at her, his hands waving and mocking her, she was certain that he hadn't ever believed her. But now he could not deny that Mahan was back.

Zinat stared at Mahan and a sudden sense of suspicion crept over her that the man sitting on the sofa beside her, staring at her with sympathy, wasn't her own Mahan. She couldn't communicate with him. She couldn't ask him whether he was hungry or thirsty or tired, as she always did. She couldn't even ask him, "Where have you been for so many years?" The words were flowing inside her like a creek, but her mouth didn't move. She might have had a stroke, she thought.

She suddenly sensed Taher sitting next to her on the sofa. "It's four o'clock in the morning. Why haven't you gone to bed? Are you feeling well? Your heart..."

How Mahan had changed places with Taher she couldn't figure out. Maybe she had fallen asleep for a few minutes. Her heart was calm, not racing anymore. Amazement was in her eyes, but Taher was indifferent to her. She stared at him without uttering one word. She couldn't tell him that he, too, must talk to Mahan and confirm that he was really their Mahan who'd come back or...

Zinat knew what Taher would say: leave aside these disturbing thoughts, take your sleeping pill and go to bed.

For years she believed she knew about things that Taher didn't know and Taher knew about the other things that she didn't know. They didn't argue with each other about the things they knew—it was useless. She was sure if she told Taher to talk to Mahan, he would shake his head and head for his room, slam the door to show his disagreement and his anger. So she chose to be quiet and say nothing.

She didn't notice when Taher finally went back to his room.

Now she was alone again with this Mahan or this strange man and she didn't know what to do with him. Whether to make him dinner or breakfast or send him to her bedroom, which actually was Mahan's bedroom, and say, "You'd better go to bed. It's late. You need to rest. I'll go to get fresh bread. Like those years when you and your sister were little and fought for having the pebble stuck to the back of bread to play with. And if the bread didn't have any pebbles, you'd make a fuss and not want to have your breakfast."

All these words were boiling in Zinat's head, but she was quiet. The morning sun lit the living room as it spilled through the kitchen window like an unwanted guest.

Taher appeared from his room. Zinat was still sitting on the sofa, lost in her reverie. Surprised, he asked, "Are you waking up now or..."

Zinat said, "Last night, Mahan..."

She didn't continue. In Taher's eyes she read a bitter pity.

The Street of Butterflies

—∿∿—

I SEE THE HOUSE THE DAY we go to look at the apartment we're going to buy. I look through the apartment's kitchen window and the house is the first thing that catches my eye. It's a bungalow on about six-hundred square metres of land. Apartment buildings flank it on either side; one with arched windows and clear glass, and the other with long, rectangular windows of pale brown glass. The apartment buildings are both much taller than the house and tower over the bungalow as if to crush it. But the house and its front yard sit solemn and proud between the buildings, as though it has been claiming its place and its dignity for a long time.

Bahman is obsessed by inspecting the apartment, determined to find problems and deficiencies. The apartment doesn't interest me at all. When Mr. Rafat opens the door and let us in, I see that it is empty. It should look spacious, but it doesn't. Thinking about fitting so much furniture in this tiny space, and about Nastaran sleeping in the same bedroom with Pouria bothers me. The kitchen is small and has only a few cabinets, though there's space for a fridge and washing machine.

I am upset. We had to sell our big house on a beautiful, green, winding street in Shemiranat, in the north of Tehran, and now I'm supposed to be happy with this tiny somewhat dreary apartment. The house belonged to Bahman's father and while Bahman's mother was alive, we lived there. Nobody ever talked about selling the house. Nastaran and Pouria were born

26

there and grew up there. They each had their own bedroom. Over time, most of the other houses in the neighbourhood were demolished and giant apartment buildings were raised in their place. The builder had offered Bahman's mother a good price, but we were lucky that she didn't permit anyone to touch the house. Two years ago, after she passed away, her daughter and son, who lived abroad, returned to Iran and claimed their shares of the estate, so we were forced to sell the house.

And now this house on the other side of street, with its white curtains, its small pond in the middle of the front yard, and its garden full of petunias, geraniums, roses bushes, and....

Bahman places his hand on my shoulder and says, "Why are you so bewitched by what is outside this apartment? We're not buying the whole street. Look at this apartment and tell me if you like it or not."

I don't need to look at the apartment. I can see everything from where I'm standing. I don't like it. This tiny apartment is in no way comparable to the large and comfortable house we had lived in for so long.

Bahman turns to me and, as if he knows what I am thinking, says, "God bless my father..."

Yes, God bless Bahman's father. We were able to pay for part of this apartment with the money we got from Bahman's share from his father's house, and the balance we were able to borrow from the bank and from some friends.

Bahman adds, "Otherwise, God knows what we would have done."

I nod and comment, "With only one of our salaries, we would never be able to afford to pay the rent for even a smaller apartment than this one."

Bahman continues, "Of course, especially as the other's salary has to be used to pay for the children's tuition." He smiles ruefully, and says, "Don't be so upset, then. Thank God, we finally own an apartment."

Nastaran and Pouria started fighting the first day we moved

to the apartment. "I won't sleep in the same room with Nastaran," Pouria insists, stamping her feet.

"I won't even let you set foot in my room," Nastaran hisses back.

We give the two bedrooms to the children and we buy a sofa bed for ourselves. At night we have to make it into a bed and in the morning turn it back into a sofa. Bahman and I have to do it by turns as soon as we get up, otherwise, it would give the children another bed to jump on.

We could only bring part of the furniture we had collected during the years living in the big house. We filled up every single bit of space in the apartment and the rest of our furniture either went into the garbage or was sold at the door for a pittance.

Our apartment building is on the Street of Butterflies in the west part of Tehran. I hear from the corner grocery store's owner that the street had once been famous for its greenness—tall, graceful trees and copious bushes of honeysuckle used to line the street. With sadness in his voice, he says, "In the spring and summer you could smell their fragrance before stepping onto the street."

When we move to this apartment, there are no signs of honeysuckle or tall trees. On both sides of the street there are only tall buildings, four-, five- or six-storeys, built in different architectural styles, different colours of brick, and different window panes. When I pass them on the street, I can see my reflection in the windows, some yellow, some brown, and some orange, and a lump in my throat goes up and down.

Bahman says, "Don't take it so hard. Thank God we have something."

I thank God for sure. I'm worried things will get worse. I saw what happened to my cousin, Pari, and her husband, who had sold their small apartment and went to the bank to get a loan to buy a bigger apartment. Prices had jumped so high that they couldn't afford to buy something similar to their previous place. So Pari had to go back to her mother-in-law's, and rent two rooms in her small house in a neighbourhood she didn't like at all. Since then she is always getting sick. She told me that she has to take pills every night to be able to sleep. So, I am very lucky compared to many people. Bahram is right. I shouldn't take it so hard. I have to thank God.

We settle in the apartment and get used to the lack of space. Actually, I don't, but Bahman and the children seem to.

And now, my only joy is to watch the house that sits across the street from our kitchen window. It reminds me so much of the house we used to live in the green valley north of Tehran. Soon after moving into the apartment, I'd spotted the family name on a blue tile, on the right side of the door, mounted on the brick wall: "Mahmood, Pirasteh."

Little by little, I discover that Mrs. Pirasteh is a lonely woman. Her two sons live out of the country and only come to visit once a while. I've seen her in her yard. She has long hair, usually braided and wrapped on top of her head. She is a tall, stout woman, a little bent when she's walking. I can't guess how old she is from this far, but it's clear that she's elderly. She wears a long dress and a big scarf covers her shoulders, but not her hair. It seems that she doesn't care about the neighbours living in the apartment buildings on the other side of her house. The house with its curtains drawn reminds me of a short story by William Faulkner, "A Rose for Emily." I talk to Bahman about it, and he says, "You are happy with your fantasies about this house."

I say, "Yes, I am."

Mr. Salamat, the owner of the corner grocery store, is one of the oldest residents on the street and his store provides many of the street's residents' needs. He has sparse salt-and-pepper hair, and he always wears a white shirt. When he speaks, he won't look in your eyes. He's usually taciturn and often won't answer any questions. I hear from his son, Nasser Agha, who runs the store when his father is away, that they converted their four-hundred-square-metre house to a five-storey apartment building. Now his parents, his other two brothers, and Nasser himself all live there with their families.

All the side streets of Safa Street are named after martyrs, such as Martyr Modarresi, Martyr Golparvar, Martyr Salehi, Martyr Manizadeh. And then there's the Street of Butterflies.

I asked Naser Agha, "Why wasn't this street named after a martyr? Hasn't it had any martyrs?"

Naser doesn't have more information about the history of the street, or if he has, he doesn't want to share it with me, an intrusive newcomer to this neighbourhood. Maybe he imagines I am an informant looking to collect information about the people that live here. He ignores me and makes himself busy with other customers.

I'm hurt by Naser Agha thinking of me as a stranger or an informant. I buy milk, honey, yogurt, and cheese, and go home. When I have a chance, I sit by the kitchen window and watch the house. I feel lucky that my view is not blocked. The house, the azure sky above it, and a small portion of the Darakeh Mountains, their summits covered by a delicate snow, fill my eyes.

Every day, when I return from work, I remove my mantou and scarf, which are like an extra layer of skin on my body, and walk to the window and peer at the house on the other side of street, as if to ensure it has not disappeared while I wasn't home. Since I know that the owner is an old woman and have heard that her sons live out of the country, I have a constant fear that she will die and her sons will come back, sell the house, and that the new owner will demolish it and build a high-rise in front of my kitchen window, blocking my view. I can't bear the thought that the small part of the sky and mountains visible behind the house might one day be stolen from me.

Last week, as I was closing the sofa bed, I felt a sharp pain in my lower back. My doctor prescribed a week of rest. We don't open and close the sofa bed any more. Bahman sleeps on the sofa without making it into a bed, and I sleep on the floor. As folks say, "Life goes on." And as our great Ferdousi says, "Sometime on the saddle and sometime under the saddle."

Today I feel better and sent Bahman to buy some vegetables. It's been a while since I've made *ghorme sabzi* for my children. I spread a few pages of newspaper on the kitchen table and start to clean the vegetables.

Once in a while, I look out of the window and watch the house. I see Mrs. Pirasteh coming out of the house. She is wearing a mantou dress for outside and a scarf over her head. A black purse is hanging from her shoulder. It's clear that she's going somewhere. I don't know why, but I suddenly grab a chador from the hook by the door, climb hurriedly down the stairs without waiting for the elevator, and run out into the street to greet her.

Mrs. Pirasteh is locking the gate in front of her house when I reach the street in front of our building. As she finishes, she turns around and starts to walk hesitantly toward me. I smile and say hello. She looks at me for a while, seemingly puzzled, so I greet her again. I introduce myself and add that I live on the fourth floor of this building and that it's been three weeks since we moved to this street.

I don't get a reaction from her. It's as if she's saying, wherever you live, it's none of my business.

Frustrated, I blurt out, "I heard you're living by yourself. If you need any help…"

Then I wonder why I said this. With a full-time job and two children, I don't have time enough even for my own chores. I'm always short of time. How can I help her? She looks at me, confused, and says nothing.

This time, ashamed, I say, "Forgive me for intruding. I thought as a neighbour…"

She stares at me and I assume she must think I'm a lunatic. Maybe she wonders why I am spying on her. But then she says,

"I am happy and surprised." She pauses and then I wonder, too. Why happy and why surprised?

"After many years living on this street," she adds, "I am surprised, and pleased, to be greeted by one of the new residents and asked how I am. So many of the previous residents have moved or passed away or are getting old like myself." With a smile full of kindness, she continues, "I'd love to visit with you. I'm mostly at home. Please, come to my place whenever it suits you. We can have tea together. You can bring your children, too, if you have any. They can play in the yard."

Mrs. Pirasteh's voice is welcoming and warm and like my grandmother's, gentle and accepting. She arranges the purse on her shoulder, pulls her scarf up and says, "If you like, tomorrow afternoon is a good time for me."

I feel like a person who's been invited to the house of God. I suggest, "After the children are back from school...?"

She smiles and nods, "Very well." And she leaves me by my door. Her steps are steady, as if she's carrying the passage of many difficult years on her shoulders.

The whole next day, I watch the house, worried that Mrs. Pirasteh will forget about our appointment and leave. I didn't get her telephone number so I can't call her. When the children come back from school, I cannot wait any longer. I help them change out of their school uniforms and have them wash their hands and faces. I pull out their bikes from among the things we have stored on the balcony and leave the apartment. In the past three weeks, whenever the children asked if they could go out onto the street to ride their bikes, I have not let them. How do I dare let two small children, only eight and ten, ride bikes on the street where cars drive by so fast?

I have baked two cakes, one with raisins, the other with walnuts. I take half of each for Mrs. Pirasteh.

I ring the doorbell and a few minutes later I hear her voice through the speaker. The gate clicks open. I send the kids in first with their bikes and then I follow them into the yard. It seems bigger and greener from close up. The vine-covered trellis creates a patch of shade in front of the door. I imagine that some time ago, a car had been parked there. Mrs. Pirasteh is standing on the veranda and invites us in.

It's the middle of the fall but the trees still have leaves though some yellow ones are scattered in the garden and in the shallow pond where a few goldfish swim. The garden isn't as lush as it seems from my kitchen window, but the petunias and geraniums are still blooming. In one part of the garden, there are several bushes of red, yellow, and green tomatoes.

Nastaran and Pouria stand by the pond and watch the goldfish. Pouria says, "They're like the fish we used to have in our pond at the other house."

Nastaran continues, "I wish we had brought them here."

Ms. Pirasteh invites me and the children inside for sweets and tea. My walnut cake and raisin cake will be served. Ms. Pirasteh also has fruits and pastries on the table.

We're sitting in a small room with a big window overlooking the yard. After the children have their cakes and tea, they go outside to play. From where I'm sitting, I can watch them exuberantly riding their bikes in the yard, expending their childish energy. I feel sad, imagining they might be remembering the large yard of the house we used to live in north of Tehran.

The question I've had since the first day I moved to this neighbourhood comes to me. I hope it isn't intrusive. "What happened that your house was spared from becoming a high-rise apartment building?" To explain my forwardness, I continue, "I love this house. We lived in such a house until three weeks ago, but, well, we had to sell it, and I miss it."

Mrs. Pirasteh cuts a piece of cake for me and another piece for herself and says, "Yes, unfortunately, these kinds of houses are going to become historic buildings. Whenever my sons come to visit, they insist I sell the house and buy an apartment, or demolish this place and build an apartment building. And me..."

I interrupt her to say, "For God's sake, please don't do it." At the same time, I think to myself, *Please don't take away that small piece of sky and mountains over your house that I love so much.*

"I have never wanted to," she replies firmly.

I suppress my sigh of relief and we continue to chat about the neighbourhood. I am so comfortable with her that I feel as though I've known her for years, as if she were a relative. I ask her another question about something I have found curious since moving to the street. "How come this street doesn't carry the name of a martyr, like all the other streets in this neighbourhood?"

A shadow of sorrow crosses her face. She stares at me blankly, then breathes deeply, and places her cup of tea on the table. "There was a martyr that this street could have been named after—my own son," she says in a soft voice. "In fact, our neighbours suggested changing the name the street to 'Parham Pirasteh.' But my husband wouldn't let them. My husband passed away three years ago."

I am even more curious now. "How did it get this name, then? Why is it called the Street of Butterflies?"

She says, "My husband chose the name for this street. We were the one first families to build a house here. In those days, it was called "Four Metres Street," because of its width. When the city wanted to formally change the name of the street, my husband suggested '*parvaneh*,' or butterfly, and no one objected."

She laughs amiably. She has big, even teeth. Her cheeks are full—not sunken because of old age. Her eyebrows are black, but there are soft bags under her dark eyes. Her long grey hair is parted in the middle, and her braid falls loosely down her back. Her hand goes involuntarily to her heart, as if she wants to pull out a sweet memory from there. With a sad smile, she adds, "My husband was very much in love with me. He wanted the street to be named after me."

I smile, "So, then your first name is Parvaneh?"

She laughs again and nods, though tears also glisten in her eyes. Her voice breaks and she continues, "As I said, my husband was in love with me and everyone who knew us knew this, too. When my husband chose the name, I said, 'I am not the only one—there are two others named Parvaneh that live on this street—they should be consulted.' But no one objected, and the street thus became known as the Street of Butterflies."

I look at Mrs. Pirasteh in silence and my eyes move from her to a photo on the wall of a young man hanging next to a photo of an elderly man with salt-and-pepper hair, full lips, and black eyes; he must be Mrs. Pirasteh's husband. The young man resembles his mother.

She says, "That's my son, Parham. He was on the front line, fighting the Iraqis. He had only three weeks of military service left when they brought his mutilated body back to us."

I know there's nothing I can say to soothe her. I can only nod and gently squeeze her hand.

She says, "This street has had many martyrs, some lost in the war and some in...."

I want to say, "I'm so sorry," but I am mute. I brush away the tears that have welled up in my eyes.

I turn to look out at the yard so that I can hide my tears from Mrs. Pirasteh. I see the children chasing each other and giggling with abandon. I tell myself, "Play, my dears. Soon you won't have such a nice place as this one to ride your bikes."

"Excuse me for upsetting you," Mrs. Pirasteh says, "but the history of this street hasn't been always so sad." She suggests I drink my tea, which is getting cold, and she adds, "When we moved here, there was still lots of land on both sides of the street. Within a few years, young and middle-aged families joined us and the street was soon filled with houses. The yards had many beautiful trees and colourful bushes of honeysuckle. Every afternoon, especially during summer, we women sat by our doors chatting while our children played in the street. When those girls and boys grew up, some of them married each other. The disaster started after the revolution, when some of the families emigrated or sold their houses and moved to the neighbourhoods in the north of the city. The construction of apartment buildings was a like an epidemic! People needed to make money by selling apartments or they needed to make sure they had homes for their children who were growing up and needed somewhere to live—just like the owner of the grocery store on the corner of the street. As you can see, mine is the only house left on this street. And who knows what will happen after my death…"

I cut short her words and say loudly, "I hope I never see that day."

Mrs. Pirasteh and I become close, almost like a mother and daughter. Many afternoons, especially in spring and summer, after my children are back from school and I have tidied up the apartment and made dinner, I visit her. Sometimes I take her a dish and sometimes she prepares one for me. She often says, "The woman who works outside the home doesn't have time to make *koofteh* or cutlet and ash." I visit with her at least three or four times per week and she's present at many of our family gatherings. Once in a while, she tells me "I wish all the neighbours were like you."

Mrs. Pirasteh never suggests that I might need her as much as she might need me to fill her loneliness. But I tell myself, that as much I need and enjoy her company, I need her house, with the moutains behind it, and the blue sky above it, just as much.

This happy time comes to an abrupt end. It's been three years since we moved to the Street of Butterflies. Mrs. Pirasteh's house, the mountains behind it, the blue sky above it, still make living in this tiny and dingy apartment bearable. As the children grow, it seems our space is getting smaller and smaller. We're in the middle of the fall and there are still leaves on trees and flowers and vegetables in Mrs. Pirasteh's gardens. It's a

Friday morning. We haven't had our breakfast yet when I hear the sound of *"La elaha el lalah"* from the street. I rush to the kitchen window and see a coffin carried by a few men from Mrs. Pirasteh's house to a hearse parked in the street. A few women and men dressed in black are following the coffin. In an instant, Bahman and I are at the door, then following the hearse by car to Beheshte Zahra.

And now Mrs. Pirasteh's sons are here. There are goings and comings at their house. I'm sure I will hear soon that the house has been sold, and there will be the sound of demolition and then the construction of another tall apartment building. God knows how long we will suffer from the noise and chaos in the street. The thought of the house being demolished is like a terrible disease, with me day and night.

One day, coming back from work, I see Mrs. Pirasteh's older son outside the house. I met him at his mother's memorial. When I walk over, he thanks me for being a friend to his mother. "My mother always talked about you," he says. Then he adds, "She said that you filled her loneliness." He tells me how often they begged her to join them in America, but she always refused, insisting that she had a good neighbour watching over her.

I wait until he finishes, then ask, "Are you going to sell the house?" The question has been with me since Mrs. Pirasteh's death.

Looking surprised, he replies, "No, we can't."

Joy makes my heart beat faster in my chest. I ask, "Then what?"

Right away I regret my abrupt question. Mrs. Pirasteh's son must think I am a terribly rude person.

Instead, in his face I see pride mixed with sadness. He says, "My father willed the house to my mother. Normally, after my mother's death, the house would go my brother and me. But my mother's will stated that she would like the house to be kept as it is, and given to a kindergarten."

My heart is beating even faster now. *Is it possible?* I ask myself.

Mrs. Pirasteh's son notices the astonishment in my eyes and continues, "My mother did not want her house to be sold or destroyed. She used to say, 'I had happy and sad times in this house and I don't want those memories to be transformed into dust.' So she wanted it to be filled with the happy laughter of children."

I tell the story to Bahman with tears in my eyes. Bahman says, "Now that your prayer has being answered, you should take a bouquet of flowers to Mrs. Pirasteh's grave every week."

Once again I remember Faulkner's story, "A Rose for Emily." I smile at him and reply, "I don't think I need to take flowers for Mrs. Pirasteh to Beheshte Zahra every week. Her garden is always full of beautiful flowers; that is enough for her, and for me."

Soleiman's Silence

—ຫນ—

WHY DID ALL IRANIANS in Toronto know Soleiman? Nobody knew. Soleiman wasn't wealthy; he wasn't a poet, a writer, a musician, or a singer. He didn't boast university or scientific titles. Soleiman was an ordinary person who chose to be silent. But Soleiman's silence spoke volumes and people read words into his silence. Some believed Soleiman had never opened his mouth to speak. He was always quiet when they saw him. But it wasn't true. Other had heard him tell the story of his past, a past as mysterious as his silence.

Some believed Soleiman was raised in a city at the edge of the desert, a city full of impatient, gloomy, and thirsty people. A city imprinted in Soleiman's face and eyes. Soleiman had told many stories about the city's long, burning, boring summers—bittersweet stories. People retold these stories in Soleiman's presence with the hope that he would confirm or deny them. He listened and said nothing.

Others believed Soleiman came from a mountainous area. They believed they had heard Soleiman describe the cold winter, gusting winds, hardworking people who didn't think about anything but how to conquer the summit hidden under the clouds. It seems that Soleiman had nice memories of this city, unlike the desert city that dragged energy from people, that made people struggle. The mountain, which sheltered the city, frightened people. The people believed there was a monster hidden on the summit of the mountain, a monster that should be killed. People worried about climbing the mountain, reaching its summit, and finding the monster that threatened them.

Others thought Soleiman was from a city in the North, close to the Caspian Sea. They said that Soleiman had described tall poplars, willows, cedars, and plane trees whose brimming greenness in summer was like a wavering hallucination in the desert. The winter was rainy, days turning quickly to night filled with dreams and memories. Soleiman spoke so elegantly about this city, that listeners could feel the breeze passing over their skins and hear the waves that crashed on its shores.

Everyone who knew him believed Soleiman was a good listener. Many witnessed the hours he spent by the lake at the south end of the city, listening to the waves or the sea gulls that careened and screeched over the lake's rocky shore. When he strolled in the lush parks of this city, he sometimes stopped walking to listen to bird songs or to the gentle whisper of the breeze. At those moments, there was ecstasy in his eyes, excitement at the sounds of the day that enveloped him. So Soleiman wasn't deaf or mute; many had heard him speaking, many had listened to his stories as well.

So why did Soleiman choose silence? It was a mystery. Even though people didn't know why, they wouldn't admit it. They considered their own lack of knowledge a fault, so every one claimed that they knew why, everyone had their own reasons to explain the mystery; reasons that might have had nothing to do with Soleiman's silence at all.

Some believed Soleiman was bored by living in exile, that he was homesick. These people had strong reasons for their own silence, but not for Soleiman's silence. They believed that exile pushes people into isolation, seclusion, and finally, and inevitably, to silence.

More than a few believed Soleiman chose to be silent because he hadn't been able to learn the new language. These people attributed their own problems to Soleiman, and cried sincerely for him. But a wise person knew these were crocodile tears.

Soleiman's problem, if he had one at all, wasn't that he didn't know the language. He could speak the language before he left Iran; in fact, he had started learning it in kindergarten. On arrival, he had a little trouble understanding the language because of the common accent, but when he heard the words clearly, he had no problem with comprehension. Soleiman's enigma wasn't language. Furthermore, Soleiman had lived in this country for years. He had attended school, learned new skills, and worked in this country. He had relationships with people of this country. There'd also been TV—his companion, night and day. Many remembered that Soleiman had listened carefully to the news, and read the newspapers. Soleiman wasn't illiterate in English.

But if Soleiman chose to be quiet, other people, people who liked to comment on everything, spoke too much. They made such a fuss, filling the air with busy words, so that even the most patient became impatient and urged them to be quiet. These busy bodies talked and talked about Soleiman's silence. Sometimes they spoke of it right in front of him. He heard them and, strangely, didn't react.

Some people believed Soleiman needed to see a psychologist or even a psychiatrist. He might have a complex of some kind, something that forced him to be silent. A psychologist or a psychiatrist might help. Perhaps Soleiman was mentally ill; maybe, he couldn't assimilate in the exile society. But these people forgot that Soleiman had been living in exile a long time and that he had suddenly chosen to be silent. In answer to these people, others claimed that Soleiman was an egoist and too proud. They said words are the only way to forge relationships among human beings. If someone doesn't answer questions, or remains silent around others, it means he doesn't respect them. For these, there is no viable reason to leave questions unanswered. These people believe human beings are talking animals. One who doesn't speak denies humanity. These people ignored Soleiman. They were hurt by Soleiman's silence. They even wished him dead because Soleiman's silence was an insult to all people who liked to offer their opinions on every aspect of life.

One thing was clear, no one really knew the real reason for Soleiman's silence. Soleiman, like all immigrants, left his own homeland and landed in this city, thousands of kilometres away from the place he called home. Soleiman once spoke like others did. He laughed, cried, joined in discussions. Some said he told good jokes and made people laugh, that he talked about his memories and his family. Now, nobody knew what had happened to them, really, and they gossiped about this in different ways because Soleiman said nothing about this either. What had happened to Soleiman? Why had he suddenly become quiet?

Iranians in the city didn't stay quiet about Soleiman's silence. They continued to express their opinions on his silence at any gathering. Sometimes this discussion would become so heated the even the most patient people became impatient and annoyed. Interestingly, if Soleiman was present, he said nothing and showed no reaction.

Soleiman became a constant topic of discussion. As if the people around him had nothing better to do but argue about Soleiman. Strangely, Soleiman became more sullen, more reserved, more determinately silent. There were people among the immigrants who had pity for Soleiman and wanted to cure his illness, if he had one. And they kept the discussion about Soleiman heated.

It is said, that once the argument was so heated that it ended in cursing, kicking, and fighting. Soleiman had been present, watching the people fighting without reaction, when he suddenly burst into flame and in an instant was turned into a handful of ashes piled onto his chair where he had sat just a moment before. The flame lasted only a few seconds and many hadn't seen it, especially those busy fighting and disputing. Only a very few saw Soleiman transform into a ball of fire and then a clump of ashes. Those who didn't see the flames didn't believe the witnesses. These people trusted only what they saw with their own eyes. They saw the ashes, but doubted they were Soleiman's.

Again, there was much discussion. But, as the majority agreed that Soleiman had indeed been burnt to ashes, and as Soleiman was no longer ever seen at any other gathering, they thought it best to bury Soleiman's ashes. They believed if the ashes were really Soleiman's, they should be buried in the soil, as all the deceased are buried in the soil for their eternal sleep. As usual, there were different opinions on this matter. Some people said the ashes shouldn't be buried in soil, because they already had been changed to soil. According to them, it was better to scatter Soleiman's ashes in the lake at the south end of the city, the lake that gave the city its historical identity should be Soleiman's eternal home.

Others had different ideas. They said that Soleiman had spent most of his spare time in a park located in the heart of the city. They said Soleiman was familiar with all the trees, bushes, and flowers in this park, all the paths through the high and low lands of the park. They said he had spent long hours on a particular bench, dissolving his presence and memory into the trees surrounding it. They insisted Soleiman was close to the swans, ducks, geese, squirrels, and the hundreds of birds that made the park a magnificent place for him. So, they argued, it was fitting that Soleiman's ashes be spread throughout the park, some of them left on the leaves of trees, or on his favourite bench, and some strewn over the park's lake to mingle with the swans, geese, and ducks that lived there.

As no one could agree on this matter, the jar of Soleiman's ashes was left intact, moved periodically from one house to another. There were many meetings held to discuss Soleiman's ashes, and a great deal was discussed at all the meetings, but no decisions were ever made.

The presence of Soleiman's ashes bothered the residents of each house like a difficult question. For that reason, the residents of the city invited the new immigrants, who felt responsibility for any problem in the community, to attend the meetings and discuss this issue with them over the long hours of the meeting. The endless speaking and sharing of ideas had become a way of life for them, the result of an unwanted immigration to an unfamiliar land, and struggling with problems that seemed to have no answers, but appeared in different shapes and sizes, forced people to try to find solutions.

The guardian of Soleiman's ashes began to change after every meeting and each new guardian felt more responsible than the last toward the ashes. The presence of Soleiman's ashes disturbed the guardians and made them feel guilty. So each looked for a solution harder than the others and invited even more people to yet another meeting. And again, after hours of discussion and exchanging ideas, the meeting would end without agreement and sometimes with fighting and kicking. The ashes would be moved to another house.

This didn't last forever. One evening, while the ashes were being transported through the downtown, through a busy, crowded intersection where all the world's races crossed, and where many a skinny old man played trumpet on the corner, the jar of Soleiman's ashes dropped to the ground and shattered into a thousand little pieces. On each corner of the intersection there was a huge high-rise, and the wind, which always whipped through the city, was always at this corner more unbridled, slapping the faces of the pedestrians without mercy. This savage, cruel wind grasped Soleiman's ashes and dispersed them in an instant throughout the big city.

The guardians of Soleiman's ashes hurried to collect them, but they were not able to retrieve them. Some of the ashes stuck to the soles of pedestrians from all around the world, pedestrians of different races and different nationalities, who walked away unaware of the spirit they carried under their feet. And then, a heavy rain pelted the sidewalks and washed away the ashes that had stuck to the street into the sewer, then to the lake, the symbol of life in this city.

Those who had been carrying Soleiman's ashes breathed easily. They described the accident to all the immigrants in a big meeting. They believed that Soleiman's spirit had dissolved into the heart of the city, the heart of life in the city, and the heart of all races and nationalities. He was in the lake, in the high-rise apartment buildings, in the parks, and in the fields around the city. He travelled to the Pacific, to the Atlantic and to the Arctic oceans, all of which surrounded the three sides of this country, his ashes flowing in the world's waters, some perhaps even becoming frozen particles encased in ice atop the world's mountains.

Yes, it was like that. And the story of Soleiman and his reasonable or unreasonable silence is still a mystery to our immigrant community.

The original version of this story appeared in a collection of short stories, Let Me Tell You Where I've Been, *published by the University of Arkansas Press in 2006.*

Flecia

—〰—

I T WAS A YEAR AGO that Kiumars introduced Flecia to us. We were three single men who got together every Friday night at Happy Hours Restaurant, where we enjoyed spending a few hours together. Kiumars had separated from his wife a few months before. I had been living by myself for a year since Mahnaz had left me. Ahmad, too, was living separately from his family, and his wife had filed for divorce. We had sworn not to marry again or have families. We seemed happy and our lives were full. I had my job in government administration and it wasn't bad compared to Kiumars's and Ahmad's. Kiumars was still working as the superintendent in a large apartment building in one of Toronto's rich neighbourhoods. He claimed they paid him like they would an engineer; actually, he was an engineer. Ahmad was a chief economist and had worked for the government in Iran, but here he drove a taxi and always complained about the nature of his job— dealing with people who had come from all around the world and didn't know how to speak English properly. Well, I took some computer courses after I arrived in Canada, and even while I was employed, I continued to upgrade my skills. This is what you need to do in this society. Thanks to Mahnaz who worked the night shift in a coffee shop and supported me. Yes, one must improve one's knowledge and skill in order to integrate into this society and get what one really deserves. If Kiumars and Ahmad fell behind, I believed it was their own fault. Unlike them, their wives learned quickly what to do and got what they were looking for. And perhaps because of that they couldn't get along with their husbands and chose to go their own way.

For me it was different. I can say for sure it was Mahnaz's fault. First, she didn't want children. She wanted to finish her education, then think about whether she wanted to have children or not. If she'd had children, she wouldn't have bothered me so much: she'd have been busy with one or two children so I could have spent my free time outside the house as I liked. Instead, when we arrived in Canada, she not only found a job in a donut shop, but she also went to school to learn English. Then she was accepted at the university. I said, "What's the use of going to university? If you had in mind to continue your education, why did you marry me?" She said, "There's no contradiction between marrying you and continuing my education."

Anyway, my problem is different from Ahmad and Kiumar's. They have children and therefore they have responsibilities. Yes, it's the women's fault, too. Though the men aren't flawless. For example, Kiumars' wife, Soori. She was an obedient, contented woman, and she loved Kiumars for sure. He complained that she didn't get along with him. But, I believed Soori when she said Kiumars wasn't an easy man to get along with.

I wondered how and when Kiumars got to know Flecia. One Friday, Kiumars didn't show up, and he didn't call either to tell us he wasn't coming. Ahmad and I waited for him for more than an hour. We drank two bottles of beer and smoked several cigarettes, but there was no sign of him. We had our dinner, paged through the Iranian newspapers, read a few articles, and commented on them. We exchanged community and world news. I asked about Taraneh, Ahmad's wife, and his children. Ahmad said Taraneh had gotten a full-time job and now he had to pick the children up after school and take them home.

I asked, "Don't you want to go back to your wife?"

"No," he said. "Taraneh isn't the same person anymore. We are like two strangers now."

"Not even for your children?" I said. "Don't you think that your children suffer when other children talk about their fathers?"

"Don't worry about my children. More than half of their classmates have separated parents; this is not unusual."

"I'm happy that I don't have children," I said. "I mean, Mahnaz didn't want to. She's going to the university and wants a degree. It's different here. We can't understand our women anymore. My sister was pregnant two months after her marriage and she gave birth to three children in four years."

"I also don't recognize my own wife anymore," Ahmad sighed. "She's changed a lot. I wonder what happened to her. She used to love me dearly. If I didn't get home till two o'clock in the morning, she wouldn't have dinner or go to bed. She used to wait up for me. And now she's somebody else—she's a stranger to me."

"It's because of this society," I said. "This society gives them too much freedom."

"But this society is not bad for you," he said. "You take advantage of your freedom."

"I am a man," I said.

"I know," he said. "Well, women probably think the same. Here, women know about their rights and don't feel they're less than men."

"You mean we should give our wives permission to take advantage of the same freedom as we have?" I asked.

"They don't need permission from us," he said. "They know their rights better than we do."

"Taraneh, too?" I asked.

"She has a boyfriend from the Ivory Coast."

"A boyfriend? I can't believe it."

He sighed again and said nothing.

That night I couldn't sleep. I wondered what I would do if

Mahnaz got involved with another man. Well, yes, she had filed for divorce and we will be going to court in three months. But still. It doesn't feel right to me.

During the week I called her several times and asked her if she was seeing another man. I knew that she was not interested in dating Iranian men. She told me many times that she would flee from Iranian men because she considered them perverts; as soon as a woman says hello, they want to drag that woman to their beds, even if only in their imaginations.

I said, "Do you believe the way these civilized Canadians think or live is better than our way? They go to bed and have sex, even when they've only just met each other. At least we Iranians make love in our own minds."

She interrupted me, "But Iranian men all have a complex and they are difficult to deal with."

Our arguments always reach a dead end. She usually says that I am taking advantage of the freedom I have here, and will go to bed with any women who is available. Her proof is the time she found out about my affair with one of my colleagues. We had a big fight about that and she left me soon afterward.

To tell you the truth, I was fed up with Mahnaz. It's true that a married man has more prestige in the community and is accepted among his peers better than a single man, but family life should have some rules. My wife didn't get home till late at night. Whenever I asked her where she'd been, she said she was either in the library or that she'd been in a class. I asked her why she couldn't study at home. She said she couldn't concentrate at home, what with the housekeeping, cooking, cleaning, and then me, and the damn TV. These things would not let her focus on her reading. Well, think about it: I had a wife but she either wasn't home and, when she was, her head was in a book. So when she said, "We'd better separate," I agreed without any hesitation, even though it was hard for me to learn to deal with the chores. I mean, although my wife had to go to school, I always had a hot meal, my clothes were washed and ironed, my bed was made, and the apartment was clean and everything was in order. I can't deny it—she looked after our home well. You should come and see what a mess it is now.

"What about your girlfriend?" Ahmad asked. "Doesn't she help you with housekeeping?"

"Are you kidding me? My girlfriend won't bother herself to clean my place. And if it isn't in tidy when she visits, she makes fun of me."

"What about you?" I asked.

"No girlfriend for me. I am not in a mood to have a girlfriend."

"Let's see…" I teased, "you're waiting for Taraneh."

"Don't talk about Taraneh anymore. She's finished for me."

Well, it was hard for him that his wife was friendly with another man. It was hard for me, too.

The next week Flecia joined our group. We weren't supposed to invite our girlfriends to our Friday night gatherings, but Kiumars brought her, explaining that she wanted to get to know his friends. She was one of those rare persons who radiate love. To get to know us, she asked simple questions: *Do you like Canada? What do you do for living? Do you have family here?* And after a short while, it was as if we had all known each other for years. The conversation flowed and familiarity warmed up our words. When she found out Ahmad and I were also separated from our families, her eyes filled with sympathy and compassion. Whenever she looked at us, she made us hot with love. The talk changed quickly to topics such as racism, culture, history, the environment, the economy, and politics. Flecia had such broad knowledge of these subjects that the three of us felt ignorant compared to her. Of course, when we still lived in our homeland, we considered ourselves political and social justice activists, and we claimed we were challenging our government to provide a better life for our all people. But when we found out we were in danger, we preferred to flee rather than to stay and continue our efforts.

Flecia spoke to us like an economist, a society and cultural specialist, and an environmentalist. She bewitched us with her original ideas, her natural beauty, and her unique character. I was fascinated by her. When I noticed Kiumars looking at me with threatening, warning eyes, I remembered that I had to be careful with my behaviour. Iranian men do not tolerate other men paying too much attention to, or flirting with, their mothers, sisters, wives, daughters or girlfriends. But I was captivated by Flecia and I had to work hard at controlling my enthusiasm in her presence.

When Flecia asked us about our origins, we boasted about how as Iranians we were from a "pure" race, by which we meant Aryan. She laughed loudly, as if she had heard the funniest joke, and said, "I don't believe that at the threshold of the twenty-first century, at the beginning of the third millennium, there's one person on the whole earth who's racially 'pure'. I think to find such a person you'd have to go to the depths of Brazil's or Australia's forests."

The three of us looked at her bewildered. Frankly, her words were insulting. I couldn't bear a woman like Flecia humiliating us in front of her boyfriend, who was Iranian like we were. I asked, "Well, what about you? You don't look like you are from a pure race."

She laughed again, seductively. Her white teeth were like pearls. Her red tongue touched the tip of her mouth, her big, dark eyes, which were not black nor brown nor even grey or blue or green, but a mixture of all colours, were wet with tears of laughter. Her exquisite eyes were wild with surprise and her cheeks glittered with freshness. Her hair reminded us that one of her ancestors, perhaps long ago, had been black. It was like a forest that no human being had touched; it didn't fall on her shoulders, but stood up on her head like a crown of golden-brown curls. And it seemed that Flecia did nothing to tame it. Her hair was the first thing that attracted the eyes; it was like a halo around her beautiful face.

"Me?" she replied mischeviously. "You won't believe me, and you may think I'm boasting, but I am a mixture of all races."

Kiumars looked at Ahmad and me and beamed with pride. He had his arms around Flecia's shoulders, and every now and then he kissed her. He was ensuring that both of us were well aware that she belonged to him.

Ahmad asked, "How do you know that?"

Flecia laughed again. Her laughter was like a spring rain that pours down suddenly after a long drought and fills you with joy.

"How do I know?" she said. "I have a family tree. A very long family tree that goes back seven generations."

"Really?" I said. There was doubt in my voice that Flecia quickly grasped.

"I knew you wouldn't believe me. But I have the blood of all races in my veins. And because of that I'm familiar with all people of the world."

Kiumars encouraged her: "Tell them about your ancestors. Don't worry if they don't believe you."

"I believe everything you say," I responded in an apologetic tone.

"Well, in brief," she said, "my seventh ancestor was a black man who was stolen from Africa, chained and beaten, kept hungry, and taken to the America as a slave. He was the father of the father of the mother of the father of the father of the mother of my mother."

I was confused and I wanted to ask Flecia to explain this more clearly, but she was so absorbed by her ancestors' story that I forced myself to listen and not interrupt with questions.

She continued, "That pure black African married a woman who had been the child of a black girl who had been raped by a white man. My sixth ancestor, who considered himself a black man even though he was of mixed race, raped a white woman and was lynched."

She looked at us, her eyes wide, and asked, "Do you know what 'lynch' means?" And without waiting for us to reply, she gave us a long lecture about how black people were hung from trees by white mobs.

Again, she didn't give us a chance to open our mouths. She continued, "That white woman found out she was pregnant, fled to an Aboriginal community, and gave birth to my fifth ancestor. My fifth ancestor married an Indian man. Their son, my fourth ancestor, married a white woman, and their son was my third ancestor. He married a Chinese woman. Their daughter was my second ancestor, who was my grandmother, and she married a European. Their daughter married a man from India and I am their child." Cool and relaxed she added, "You see, this is me, made of seven different ingredients." And again she laughed.

"You see," Kiumars said, "Flecia is the symbol of all races and now she's going to mix with someone of the Aryan race."

"Aryan race? I haven't heard of such a thing," Flecia said, surprised. "Did you invent such a race?"

"How haven't you heard about the Aryan race?" Ahmad said. "Hitler, in Germany, claimed it was the superior race."

Flecia's eyes widened with disbelief. "And he was responsible for the most heinous acts! Are you sure you want to say that you are from the Aryan race?"

"We are indeed Aryan," I said. "Hitler's concept of the Aryan race was quite different.... Our Aryan roots derive from our ancient Indo-Iranian origins."

Flecia nodded and then we debated history, the intermingling of races, cultures, and societies for many hours on many evenings. We enjoyed Flecia's cascading laughter and intimate manner, which was like spring sunshine that warmed and delighted us. We always had wonderful and memorable evenings when Flecia joined us.

A few months passed and Flecia broke up with Kiumars. She told me he expected too much from her. We talked on the phone a few times, and then one day she said she wanted to visit me at my place. She stayed for the night.

Kiumars stopped talking to me; Ahmad too. They said I had double-crossed them. But it wasn't my fault. I couldn't refuse Flecia's friendship and send her back to Kiumars. He wasn't worthy of her. Flecia was an exceptional woman, warm and full of love and compassion. Knowing her was a privilege for me; she helped me to understand women better. I learned a lot from her about the secrets of womanhood. She even helped me to reconsider my relationship with Mahnaz. Through Flecia, I realized that Mahnaz had been a devoted wife, a wife who loved me, but she was also keen to learn and grow as a person, and I had ignored her.

Flecia used to say, "I'm like the earth, accepting and giving." And she really was. Her ideas about race, about life, thrilled me and made me rethink my own notions about the mixing of races and about our expectations of women. I was close to falling in love with her when she left me.

I called Kiumars and told him, "Flecia left me. Don't be angry with me. Let's be friends again."

"You deserved that," he said. "When you steal your friend's girlfriend, you should be punished the same way."

"I didn't steal her," I said. "She came to me."

"Why didn't she go to Ahmad?"

"I don't know," I said.

Several weeks passed and the coldness between us began to fade. I called Kiumars and Ahmad and asked if we could resume our Friday night get-togethers. It was the second or third week when Flecia joined us again, this time with Ahmad. Neither Kiumars nor I were surprised. We welcomed Flecia enthusiastically. As usual, she warmed our gathering with her laughter and her discussion of whatever was the topic of the day. Being with Flecia seemed to eliminate any animosity among us.

After a few months, Flecia left Ahmad, too, and the three of us never got together again on Friday nights.

Later, I learned Kiumars had gone back to his wife. There was no news from Ahmad. I went to Happy Hours two or three times, but I never saw him there. I called him once to see how he was and he told me he needed to spend more time with his children. I asked if Taraneh had remarried.

"No. That man was only a friend, a colleague," he said. Then he added, "I'm actually thinking of going back to my family."

I felt lonely. I called Mahnaz and asked her how she was doing. A few months had passed since the appointment regarding our divorce. I had completely forgotten about it and so had Mahnaz. Another time was set and we arranged a meeting to decide how to divide our belongings. On my way there, I never imagined that I would go back to my wife, but I did.

Now, Kiumars, Ahmed and I occasionally get together with our families and sometimes we talk about Flecia. Incredulous, our wives listen to us talking and ask, "Are you sure you aren't dreaming? Did such a woman really exist?"

And we ask ourselves, "Did she?"

The French Fiancé

—∿—

"YOU TOLD ME THAT your fiancé was French," Nahid said. She was driving fast along a highway that glowed under the streetlights, fading in the morning light. There had been mostly silence between them during the trip from the airport to home.

When Nahid repeated her comment, Azar answered boldly, "Yes, he was." And then she turned to fix her gaze outside the window. There were no more words exchanged after that.

At home, Nahid led Azar to a bedroom that had been readied for her, and then she made her way to the kitchen to start breakfast and put on a pot of tea.

Azar closed the door of the bedroom quietly and joined her in the kitchen. She held a wet diaper and asked Nahid, "What can I do with this?"

Nahid took a plastic shopping bag from a drawer and handed it to Azar. "Put the diaper in this and dump it in the garbage."

"You don't recycle it?"

"What?"

Azar tucked the diaper into the bag and looked around for the garbage can. Nahid seemed exasperated. She took the bag from Azar, opened the door of the cabinet under the sink, and dumped the bag into the trash. She washed her hands and said, "I made fresh tea for breakfast. Pointing to a room on the left of the kitchen, she said, "There's the washroom if you want to wash your hands." While Azar was in the washroom, Nahid stood by the kitchen window, her face stern and unsmiling. The morning light coloured the building on the other side of the alley like a delicate fog and she didn't notice when Azar returned. When she turned around, Azar was once again sitting down at the table. Nahid walked over to the stove, poured the tea into two big glass cups, and placed them on the table. "You must be very tired," she said.

Azar leaned forward, and asked, "Is Mr. Engineer sleeping?"

"No, he's on a trip, to Zahedan and Kerman, those areas. He is mostly not at home. He's interested in exploring Iran. Thank God…"

She trailed off and sipped her tea. Tired, Nahid didn't have any appetite for breakfast. She had been awake the whole night. She had been anxious about seeing her sister and had tossed and turned for hours. She had driven to the airport at two o'clock in morning. Nastaran had wanted to go with her, but she dissuaded her, suggesting that she come with her children to see her aunt later in the afternoon.

Azar put a morsel of bread and cheese in her mouth. She didn't have any appetite either. She'd had food twice on the plane. "Our breakfast, when Maman was alive," she said with a trace of sorrow in her voice. "Do you remember? She always woke up early in the morning…"

Nahid didn't answer. She looked directly into Azar's eyes and began to say something. "Azar…" she uttered, but then didn't continue.

Azar stared at her and said, "What is it? Is it the baby?"

Nahid said, "Yes, why…?"

Azar didn't let her finish her words. "I know. It's because he's black?"

Nahid said, "Well, yes. You said your fiancé was French. You said his name was Alen and…"

Azar had another morsel of bread and cheese in her hand, but she put it down and forced herself to swallow the first morsel. She placed her hands against the table, leaning in close to Nahid, and as if she needed to confirm it, she said, "Yes, I told you that Alen was French. Well, he was. His parents were French and he was born in Quebec. He wasn't as black as his son. If I had known..." She paused.

Nahid said, "If you had known what?"

Azar turned her face away from her sister, and looked out the window. The daylight was a stark fact now—almost harsh as it spilled through the window, spreading everywhere.

Nahid said, "Have you thought about it?"

"About what?"

"About our families, friends. About Nastaran and Niloofar, Mehdi and Farhad, our relatives. What do I tell them? How do I explain it to them? The worst is Mostafa. If he finds out that the child is..." she hesitated, "...an illegitimate child, he will give me, give us, a hard time."

Azar stood up. It wasn't anger that made her stand up, it was surprise. She hadn't thought at all about what Nahid was now telling her. Should she have thought about it? She had told Nahid everything and had written to her in detail as well.

"I'm so lonely, Nahid." She still could not turn to face her sister. "With a child only a few months old and the grief of Alen's death, I didn't know what to do. My life is torn apart. My psychologist told me to return to my country, to stay with my sister, that then I might forget."

Earlier, Nahid had said, "Yes, come. I'm here. I'm not dead yet. I'm lonely, too. Mostafa is mostly away. I'm not sure if he has a wife somewhere else. Even if he has, it's not important to me anymore. Well, come. What are you waiting for?"

And Azar had come.

"And now what are you going to do?" Nahid asked.

Azar sat down again. The sunlight was like an unwanted guest, blanketing the sofa in the living room, and creeping toward the kitchen. She stretched out her hand, reaching for the bread, then pulled it back. Nahid abruptly got up, poured fresh tea for them both.

"What do you suggest I should do?" Azar asked. "He's my son, Alen's son. We had planned to get married. When the accident happened, I wasn't in the car with him. I wish I had been." Her voice broke.

Nahid lightly touched Azar's arm, but said nothing.

"Then I found out, I was pregnant. I couldn't...."

"But...?" Nahid asked, her eyes narrowed, her lips tight.

"But what?"

"Didn't you think about the consequences? About today?"

"No, I didn't think about anything. If you had met him—I mean Alen..."

"But he wasn't black."

"No, he wasn't. His grandmother was black. His father, too. But his mother and his grandfather were white. Alen was mixed race."

"So, why this...?"

"This...?" Azar was confused.

"I mean, why so black?"

"How do I know? Well, the previous generations were black. I didn't order a black baby."

Nahid gave her an anxious, uncertain smile. She shook her head, and dropped her eyes, as though she couldn't imagine what might be next. Frustrated Nahid cried out, "So, tell me, tell me what must I do now?"

Azar raised her voice. "I don't understand what you mean. Over there, in Canada, I didn't have any problems, even with the Iranians who were living there. What's going on here? This child is my son. His father was my boyfriend. We were going to be married. If Alen hadn't died in a car accident, and was with me now, it wouldn't matter if my son were black or white or anything! He would have a father. Isn't that true? And now..." She stopped, got up, and began pacing the small kitchen, her arms wrapped tightly around her. "And now what? What do you expect me to do?"

Nahid also got up and turned off the lamp over the kitchen

table. "You'd better rest," she said gently. "Aren't you tired? Did you sleep on the plane?"

Azar didn't say a word. It was the first time she had been in Nahid's apartment. When she'd left Iran, Nahid and Mostafa, Nastaran, and Niloofar were living in a big house in the Vanak area. Azar had loved that house. She had swum in its pool so many times with Nastaran and Niloofar, and she'd gone with them to restaurants and the cinema. Nahid was a like a second mother to Azar. Fifteen years had passed since she had left Iran. Her parents had passed away and she couldn't come for their memorials because Mahmood had refused to give her her passport when she separated from him.

It seemed to Nahid that she didn't know her sister anymore. There was a new, big, and incomprehensible gap between them. Azar was no longer the noisy, active, happy young girl whom their mother always worried would make trouble outside of the house and be arrested by Pasdars because she was always careless with her hijab and she insisted on wearing make up.

"Don't you want to rest while the baby is sleeping?" Nahid asked again.

Then as if she hadn't heard her, Azar sat back down at the table and asked, "Do you have any news from Mahmood? I heard when Father died, he came to visit."

"Do you mean that he shouldn't have come? Father was his uncle." Nahid was glaring at her, anger twitching at her lips

Azar was glued to her seat at the table. She didn't have the energy to move.

Nahid didn't feel sleepy either. Since she had seen the baby in Azar's arms she had been disturbed. She didn't want to accept it. She was ashamed of talking about the baby, and all she wanted was to forget that he existed, but he was as real as the sunlight that streamed through the apartment and she couldn't deny that he was there, with them.

"I don't understand why you left Mahmood," Nahid said. "You seemed so much in love with him."

Azar lifted her eyes to look at her sister. She was pinching and shaping a piece of bread into a gummy ball. "You thought I was in love with him? Uncle wanted us to get married. He wanted his son to have a wife in exile and not be lonely. Baba and Maman liked it, too; they were happy to get rid of me. They were too old when they had me and couldn't take care of me."

"And you liked going to Canada."

"Yes, but I was a stupid young girl then. What can you expect from a seventeen-year-old? Why did Maman and Baba have another child when they already had three grown up children? What would have happened if they hadn't had me?"

"Complaining about the past won't solve anything. Do you think life here will be easy for you with a fatherless child?" Nahid snapped.

"Nahid, if you had lived there too, you would understand what I went through," Azar replied with a lump in her throat. Brushing away the tears that had started to spill down her cheeks, she added, "I had nobody over there, nobody, you understand? I spent ten of my best years with Mahmood. He wouldn't allow me to continue my education and finish high school. He didn't want me have a child. And he wouldn't let me get a job. And when I left, he denied me everything. I was lucky I didn't end up in a hospital. Alen helped me when I was desperate and had nowhere to go."

Nahid stood behind her, and impulsively threw her arms around her shoulders, holding her close without saying a word.

The sun now flooded the room. Nahid was wondering if the telephone would ring and if Nastaran or Niloofar would want to come to see their aunt. She said, finally, "I understand. It was hard for you. But you should have written to me sooner."

Azar answered coldly, "I didn't write to anyone, about anything. No, I didn't want to moan and beg for your help. Don't you remember, once I complained that Mahmood had insulted me, and you wrote to me saying that I had to accept his ways. Correct? So, I didn't write anymore."

Nahid softened her tone and tried to be more compassionate: "But you should have written to me about *this* much sooner."

Hurt and surprised, Azar asked, "Written to you about what?"

"About being pregnant before you were married."

And after a while she continued, "And when the boy had his accident."

"The boy! You mean Alen?"

"Yes," Nahid answered.

"Well, I did write to you, and I talked to you about it on phone."

"But you didn't tell me you were pregnant."

"No, I didn't tell you I was pregnant. I knew if I told you about it, you would encourage me to have an abortion and I didn't want that."

"What do you want to do now?"

"You tell me what should I do. This child is my son. I gave birth to him. I'm still breastfeeding him. I have an Iranian birth certificate and an Iranian passport for him. I wanted to bring him Iran to introduce him to his relatives. And now you're suggesting..."

Azar got up from the table, went to the living room and sat on a big sofa. Outside the window, two tall buildings blocked her view. The sun dipped behind a cloud and the room suddenly seemed dark.

Nahid sat on the edge of a sofa as if she had something urgent to do and was poised to get up and leave. She was restless and anxious. She looked at the clock on the wall and the narrow ray of sunlight that was making its way back into the apartment. She couldn't see the sky beyond the buildings outside her living room window, but she could smell the air pollution that would get denser as the day progressed. With sadness and disappointment in her voice, she said, "Azar jaan, don't be upset with me."

But Azar raised her voice involuntarily and said, "Tell me what to do. I can't hide him. I can't kill him." She covered her face with her hands and burst into tears. Sobbing and shaking, she jumped when she heard the baby cry and rushed to the bedroom. Nahid followed her and stood by the door as Azar took the baby in her arms, opened her shirt, and tenderly held the baby to her breast. Standing by the door, Nahid thought she should hug and kiss Azar, and the baby, but she couldn't make herself step forward. The baby was like a scar in her sister's arms, and again Nahid wished he simply didn't exist.

Wiping the tears from her face, Azar watched her baby suck slowly and rhythmically.

Nahid was consumed by shame, anger, and frustration. She had to find a solution. Anxiety was like a fire burning her insides.

Azar lifted her head and looked at Nahid with tears still glistening on her cheek. "I am sorry, Nahid jaan. I didn't want to make problems for you."

Nahid tried to control her anger "I have chores to do, my dear," she replied tersely. And then she continued, "I'm sure that Nastaran, Niloofar, and their children will come to visit today. Then Mehdi and Farhad, and then others. I will have to tell them."

"Tell them? Tell them what? You mean about Alen? Or about the baby? You shouldn't tell them anything. I will tell them and answer all their questions. You don't need to worry."

"You will tell them? What do you want to tell them? For example, what will you say to Mostafa? If you only knew how hypocritical he is! If he learns that you are not married, he will make sure that I am disgraced in front of everyone like a worthless penny."

The baby let go of his mother's breast and looked around. He gurgled and smiled at his mother. Azar lifted him to her face and gently kissed him. She let his head rest on her shoulder and tapped lightly on his back. The baby's dark skin contrasted sharply against his mother's pale skin. Azar didn't say a word. As if she hadn't heard a word Nahid said.

"Do you remember how I took care of Nastaran and Niloofar when you and Mostafa went to Shokoofe New or Cabaret Miami or to the Caspian shore?" Azar said.

Nahid wanted to say we also took you to the Caspian shore with us, but she didn't. She wasn't in the mood to chat about the past. The past was lost somewhere, where even remembering it seemed unreal. She didn't want to get close to the baby or to hold him or hug him. The baby was a stranger to her. Azar couldn't be his mother and it wasn't clear who his father was either. It wasn't Alen. The Alen whose photo Nahid had seen bore no similarity to this six-month-old baby. He didn't look like Azar, either. Where had Azar found him? A thought lit her mind like a lightening bolt but she didn't dare voice it. Suddenly, a hint of joy lit her face. She moved closer to Azar and took the baby from her arms. The baby gazed up at her, his eyes black, wide, and innocent, and smiled crookedly at her before he began to wail. If Azar hadn't been right there, she might have imagined that Nahid had pinched him. Nahid promptly handed him back to his mother and said, "He doesn't know me yet."

Azar said, "He knows you and he is aware that he's not welcomed by you." She caressed the baby to soothe him and he quickly calmed down.

Nahid left the bedroom and turned her head to add, "I have to make something for lunch and dinner. Niloofar and Nastaran may come at any moment. You'd better rest."

Azar wondered what had happened to Nahid. Her attitude toward Azar had changed; her cheerful nature had become somber. Azar was hurt by Nahid, who had always been like a mother to her. Now she regretted returning to Iran. Since the first moment Nahid had seen the baby in her arms and realized that he had been conceived outside of marriage, her attitude had changed and there was a new coldness in her words and expressions.

Azar placed the baby on the bed and lay down beside him.

She burst into tears, but tired and frustrated, she soon fell asleep next to her infant son. When she woke, the baby was awake, too, his fingers curled into her hair.

Nahid opened the door quietly and entered the room. "You slept for two hours. Are you still tired?"

Still angry, Azar was aloof. "Yes, I slept." She sat up, looked at the baby whose arms and legs danced in the air. Azar felt her heart sink when she looked into his big, black eyes. The baby's innocent stare always made her cry and Alen's memory was like an arrow piercing her chest.

Nahid sat down beside Azar and said, "I have an idea. I mean, I have a solution." She placed her arm around Azar's shoulders with the gentleness and kindness of earlier days. "I thought we might tell Nastaran, Niloofar, and the others that this baby is your adopted child, not your real child...."

Nahid stopped abruptly and looked curiously at Azar's blank expression. It seemed Azar hadn't understood what Nahid had meant.

Azar was quiet and waited for Nahid to finish.

Nahid said, "It's not a bad idea. You won't need to explain. You know, getting pregnant before marriage..."

Azar shook her haed and said, "I don't understand at all. I explained everything to you and wrote to you. My doctor said, go to your country and be with your family and you said, come. And now..."

Nahid interrupted her and added, "It's all right with me. My problem is with Mostafa, with Nastaran and Niloofar, Mehdi, Farhad, and their relatives. I don't want my daughters to be humiliated in the eyes of their husbands and their relatives..."

"I know," Azar said, her lips tightly pursed.

Nahid hugged her and kissed her. "Try to understand my situation. Now you're in Iran, not in Canada. Here things are different. People judge you. Do you remember how strict Maman was with you? You should understand this."

"I do," Azar replied, her tone frosty.

"So, you won't mind if I tell my children that you adopted this child?" Nahid said, her voice firm.

Stunned and incredulous, Azar looked at Nahid and said nothing. Then she picked up her son and gently placed him at her breast.

A Suitable Choice

—ᴍ—

IS IT MY FAULT? No, it's not. It happened without my intention. I don't know why everyone puts the guilt on men in these situations. Why is it my fault? What did he expect from me? I wanted to collect my belongings and leave—he wouldn't let me. Well, then it happened. I didn't mean it to happen. So it's not my fault.

Is it my fault? No, it's not. Yes, I betrayed Gholam, but I didn't want to. The fact is, I didn't choose him. How could I make a choice from such a long distance? Yes, I saw his photo, and a five-minute videotape, and I talked to him on the phone, once. That's it. I just wanted to escape from that damn place. Gholam made it possible for me to do so.

Is it my fault? I don't think so. But everybody put the blame on me. Yes, I shouldn't have married a woman I didn't know well, had only seen in a photo, and talked to once in a phone call. "A big mistake," Kamyar had said. Not only Kamyar, but some of my other friends had also told me the same thing, directly or indirectly: "It might not have a happy ending."

It was my mother's fault. She came to visit me after seven years. She was shocked by my life, thought my apartment was a mess. "A pig sty," is how she described it. "Oh, my God, so many girls in Iran looking for a man like you, and you are still a bachelor? When I go back to Iran I'll do something about it –a suitable wife, that's what you need." Yes, it was my mother who sent me a wife. And now everyone thinks I am the guilty party.

What should I have done then? Gholam didn't want me to leave. We had been roommates for a while and we lived in peace and harmony. It was Sima who caused the problems. Yes, it's true that I was attracted to Sima from the moment we first met. She wasn't a very beautiful or even a good-looking young woman, but she was sweet and cordial and there was something about her that was enchanting. We became friends quickly. I couldn't believe she was raised in Iran. When I lived there, girls, women, were different. Most were shy and never got familiar with a man they didn't know. But Sima was easy-going, as if she had known me for years. How can I put it? She wasn't shy at all.

Kamyar and I became friends first. Well, I don't like building a wall between people and myself. Both came to greet me at the airport when I arrived. At first glance, I liked Kamyar, but when Gholam handed me the bouquet of flowers, I realized he was the person I would be marrying. Everybody called it "a suitable choice." What a choice! Kamyar was filming us. Gholam introduced him to me as his friend and roommate. We became friends that first night. We all lived in the same house.

She became more intimate with Kamyar than me. I was dazed and tongue-tied. I couldn't believe this educated, charming, chatty, and friendly woman was my wife. Yes, I'm not as socially comfortable with women as Kamyar is. He says, "You've imprisoned yourself in your small world: work, work, and work, nothing else. You don't read any books, you don't watch any films, and you even don't read the newspapers or watch TV." He's right, but why is that wrong? I don't have time for those things.

I believe it was Gholam's fault. I told him, don't do it, it's risky. "What's risky?" he said. "So many people get married this way. I am not the first to do this."

I told him, "There is a risk that you will not understand each other, or even like each other. How can you get to know her when she lives few thousand kilometres away, and all you have seen is a photo and a video?"

"When she arrives here, I will get to know her," he said.

"I don't think that is the right thing to do," I insisted.

Gholam said I should have learned everything there was to know about him from the five-minute videotape I was sent, and from our short telephone call. How could I? When I saw him at the airport, even at first glance, I realized he wasn't for me. If Kamyar weren't there, I might have liked Gholam, but next to Kamyar, he wasn't attractive at all. They were completely different. Kamyar was young, tall, and handsome, and Gholam was chubby, older, and almost bald. His name! Gholam! In Canada, they call him Gol. I find that terribly funny. In Farsi, "Gol" means flower! "You're my wife," he said. "You married me. You knew me."

I replied, "How could I know you? How could I know anything about you at all?"

"You chose me," he implored.

I wished I could tell him that if Kamyar had sent me his videotape I would have chosen Kamyar, but I didn't have a choice—the only videotape I was shown was Gholam's.

Yes, it was my fault, but many men marry this way and their wives turn out to be nice women and they have happy lives. It was my fault that I didn't ask Kamyar to leave my house before she arrived. To tell you the truth, I couldn't do it. We lived together for more than seven years, and we'd never had any problems. He wasn't only my tenant; he was like a brother to me, a younger brother. He cared about me. He worked nights and slept during the day and was no trouble at all. Indeed, we were good friends.

When I heard his wife was going to arrive soon, I'd said to Gholam, "I'd better move out. Not be in your way."

"No need to move out. Please stay," he'd said, sounding hurt. "You're like a brother to me. You know that."

Well, we were like brothers, I can't deny that. We never had a problem. He's a patient, generous man.

Gholam is a nice man. It's just that he's not chatty. He normally has nothing to talk about, but he's a good listener. When Kamyar is with us, I like to talk. But with Gholam I have nothing to say. It's as if the words are stuck to in my mouth and won't come out. There's a distance between us, and it is getting wider and wider. Yes, he's much older than Kamyar and me—fifteen years older. Kamyar and I are the same age. When I realized Kamyar was six months younger than me, I laughed and teased, "You're still a child!"

"What do you mean?" he said. "Then, you're a child, too!"

"No," I giggle, "I will be twenty-five before you are."

Sima and Kamyar always teased me about their age, reminding me that I'm getting old. In four months, I will turn forty. "I would never have guessed you are forty," Sima said. "You don't look like you're forty."

I said, "I am thirty-nine, I am not forty yet!"

Gholam looks like a person who has swallowed a stick: always upright, unable to laugh at any joke. Whenever we, I mean Kamyar and I, tell a joke, he shows no interest. If Gholam and I lived in Iran, with this attitude he has, I would have turned into dust by now; I couldn't bear it. Life is not only formality and morality. To be free to talk, to live and to laugh as I like were my main reasons for wanting to leave Iran; otherwise,

I would have been crazy to leave my family, my friends, and my home. We are in Canada, not in the Islamic Republic of Iran where laughter is an offence.

She's friendly, sincere, helpful, and lively. When she arrived, my friends came to visit. She entertained them with her numerous jokes. Her loud, joyful laughter was contagious and everybody enjoyed her presence. I could see my friends were envious, thinking I was lucky to have such a good wife. I wished they were right. Yes, I have a good wife, but I was not sure I could keep her—and not because I didn't want to keep her. I love her, but it seems she doesn't feel the same way about me. She is more interested in Kamyar than me.

He should have realized that Sima wasn't interested in him. They are made from different dough, completely different from each other. Even though she didn't tell me at first, later, when we were more intimate, she admitted it was a big mistake. "What do you mean—a big mistake?"

Although I knew what she actually meant, I asked, "Coming to Canada was a mistake?"

"No," she said. "Choosing Gholam as a husband was a mistake."

"Well, did you have another choice?" I asked her.

"No, there wasn't another one," she answered. "In fact, Gholam was my only choice. But I do not regret coming to Canada," she said, smiling mischievously. "Here, I have more choices."

"How come?" I asked. "Well..." she started, but stopped to polish the apple in her hand. Then she carefully peeled it, cut it in half, and gave me a piece as she bit into her piece. Her eyes were shining and as the juice from the apple dribbled slightly from the corner of her lips, I couldn't resist biting into my own piece and filling my own mouth with the apple's sweet juice. It was only a week after she'd arrived.

They were supposed to have gone on their honeymoon. But Sima postponed the trip, saying she was still tired from her long journey from Iran.

I got to know him much better on our honeymoon. He wasn't unbearable. Not a bad person, actually a good person, generous, honest. He never said "no" to me. But he is boring and dull. I don't know what he has done with his life. Yes, he's educated, has an engineering degree, and is working as a programmer. But life shouldn't be limited to work alone. On our honeymoon, I sometimes I felt I was lying next to a stone, or a statue that showed no compassion or enthusiasm for anything. I couldn't ever tell whether he was upset or happy. He never showed any emotion. It seemed he had no experience with women and didn't know anything about them. He didn't even try to get to know me, didn't ask me questions about what I like or don't like. I don't blame him for not knowing me. How could I? He sometimes stared at me as if I were a strange and alien creature. Once I asked him, "What do you see in me? Do I look bizarre to you?" He turned his eyes away from me and said nothing. He was really boring.

He quickly realized that Sima didn't like him, and thought marrying him was a mistake. Sima's silence was full of words: "What a damn choice." But in her eyes I could see there was something else glittering, as if she were asking, "Why didn't you send me a videotape and ask me to marry you? Why Gholam? If it had been you, I would have been the happiest girl in the world." Yes, everything was obvious in her eyes; I could read them clearly. I tried to avoid Sima, not to make things complicated. I stayed in my room in Gholam's absence, but temptation didn't leave me. No, it wasn't me who initiated it. She did.

I trusted Kamyar. We knew each other for more than seven

years. He always said, "You're like a brother to me." Well, I was like a brother to him. I helped him to settle when he first arrived to Canada. He was young and naïve, and he knew no one. He was a refugee claimant. When a friend of mine introduced him to me, I invited him into my home, and didn't ask him for rent until he found a job. I loved him, the way I loved my brother Nader, who lost his life for nothing. Kamyar was a good guy and he loved me, too. I encouraged him to go to university and get a degree. I told him, with only a high school diploma, you get nowhere. But he didn't show any interest in continuing his education. "Take it easy," Kamyar told me. "Life is too short."

Kamyar spent most of his spare time reading or going to movies. He dreamed of being a filmmaker and spent most of his money on films and books. He filmed us with his camera in the airport. Before Sima, we didn't have any problem with each other. Actually, because of his work schedule, we didn't see each other very often, but he was there and I had a good feeling, as if I was living with my own brother.

My mother loved him, too. He reminded her of Nader, the son she lost in the war. "If you would like, I can find you a match, too," she had said to him. "There are many girls yearning to leave Iran."

But Kamyar took it as a joke, laughed loudly and said, "No, Mother, I'm not looking for trouble."

He is young, and has plenty of time ahead of him, not like me, almost forty, almost bald, and of the few hairs that are left on my head, the grey hairs far outnumber the black ones.

It wasn't my fault it happened. I didn't want it to end like that. Yes, at first glance I wished these two could have changed places. But later ... I understood their relationship. When Gholam told me they'd been living together for more than seven years, and Kamyar was like his martyr brother, Nader, I tried to look at him as a brother, too. In the beginning, he hid himself in his room. I didn't want to go to his room but then it happened. A postman came to the door, and I didn't know the language so I had to call Kamyar for help. At other times there were phone calls, and again there was a language problem and I had to ask Kamyar for help. And after that, we would sit and talk. I was a newcomer and didn't know much about the city and life in this country. Gholam worked every day and I was at home bored. I talked to Kamyar about my life, about Iran. And he talked about his family. I was talkative when Kamyar was around.

It wasn't my fault it happened. At first I simply liked her, like a sister-in-law. I never imagined betraying Gholam. It happened. It wasn't Sima's fault, either. She was lonely and didn't love Gholam. I knew Gholam loved her. He looked at her as if she were from Venus. Sima isn't very pretty: medium height and a bit overweight; she has narrow lips, an eagle nose, and a complexion the colour of wheat. Her long face didn't match her height and her stout body. But her eyes were big, light brown, glimmering and cheerful. And she was always really happy when she was with me. At the airport, when she appeared from the transit hall, dragging her heavy bags, she greeted us as if she had known us for years. I was supposed to film them, but forgot totally about it and then I when I did film them, it was out of focus. When we watched the film afterward it was funny and we laughed. Not Gholam—he might have realized something, but what? Nothing had happened yet.

They thought I was stupid and realized nothing. They thought I was made of bricks, with no emotion. It was clear to me even that first night, when Sima mostly addressed Kamyar and compared me to him, I figured out he was the one she was attracted to. When we were alone, she asked about him, then excused herself. She didn't even undress in front of me. She changed into her nightgown in the bathroom, turned the light off, and climbed into bed. She faced the wall, her back to me, and mumbled a good night. She excused herself, saying she was tired from travelling such a long way. But I was awake the whole night, and I couldn't believe I had a woman in my bed, a goddess. Her perfume made me dizzy, but I didn't dare touch her to wake her up. She slept like a log and I had to go to work the next day. I didn't take a day off; I left it for our honeymoon.

On our honeymoon I realized I couldn't live with him. He wasn't my type. I couldn't make myself love him. I knew my parents would be hurt and would turn against me. But what could I do? I couldn't lie to myself. I told Kamyar, "I have nobody here except you. I don't love Gholam. What should I do?" He looked at me in silence. How long? I don't know.

I don't know how it happened. Yes, I liked her. I liked her from the very first night. She bewitched me. I don't know how we ended up in each other's arms and later in my bedroom. She said, "What do we do now?"

I told Kamyar, "Let's leave here. Here isn't our place anymore. I can't face Gholam. I know what I've done. In Iran, a woman who commits adultery is stoned to death."

She was terrified. She imagined she would be condemned to death. I made her understand we weren't in Iran and she was safe here, didn't have to answer to anyone except herself. I told her, I will leave this place and you will behave as if nothing has happened.

Kamyar wanted to leave me and then I would have to cope with my sin alone. I beseeched and cried, "Please, don't leave me. Aren't you in love with me?"

He said, "I am, but I love Gholam, too, I respect him, he's

like a brother to me. He has done a lot for me and I can't steal his wife from him in turn."

I told him, "We'd better talk to Gholam and then leave."

They're waiting to hear the last word from me. To hear that they can be together and go to their own way. I paid for the wedding, paid for her jewellery, paid for the ticket to bring over a wife for Kamyar. They misunderstood me. I watched them and waited to see which one would feel guilty and break first. I know Sima can't be a wife for me. But I didn't want to lose her so easily. I want her to pay for this transgression. She must feel the shame of this. She thought she could take Kamyar away from me. I had a taste of what it would be like to have a wife; to come home and find my supper on the table, my house clean, and the aroma of a woman's perfume making my legs tremble.

I look at Sima in silence and blame her without saying a word, making her feel ashamed of herself. And you, Kamyar, whenever you get close to my wife, I'll be a thorn in your eyes. Wait, and I'll show you.

When I introduced Mina to Sima, her eyes filled with tears, but she was able to keep herself from crying. I had known Mina for a few years. We were just friends and had never dated. I liked her. She was an independent woman; she lived by herself and was always busy. She's twenty-four and always said, "I don't have time for men." When I told her about Sima, she said, "You're in a big mess."

"How do I get rid of this mess?" I asked her, sincerely looking for help.

She said, "Marry me." She was serious.

I was shocked and asked, "Do you mean it?"

She replied, "Yes, of course, I love you."

Within a week, we got married at the city hall. Gholam and Sima were our witnesses. They accompanied us to the airport.

I couldn't stay in that house another minute, or even in this city any more. I couldn't do anything for Sima. She chose her husband from almost seven thousand kilometres away. Now it's up to her what she wants to do with him.

Where Is Paradise?

—ᴍᴍ—

For all those children who lost one or both parents during the eighties and in the mass executions in 1980 in prisons of the Islamic Republic of Iran.

MAMAN JAAN, IS IT TRUE that you've gone to paradise, among the stars? If that's so, why does Grandma take me to Beheshte Zahra every Thursday afternoon and sit by a grave and lament for you? I can read your name on a piece of stone: "Setareh Dadfar."

I asked Grandma why my mother's family name is different from mine and she said your mom has her own father's family name and you have yours. Where is my father anyway?

I haven't seen you to be able to tell you that since you sent me home with Grandma, Ammeh Pooran came to visit and took me to Khanum jaan's place. But I didn't see my Baba jaan there. When Khanum jaan saw me, she hugged me and wailed loudly. I asked for Baba jaan. Khanum jaan said, "Your Baba jaan is in paradise." So, are you both together in paradise?

You know, Maman jaan, when I was with you in Evin, I was so happy. I had many *khalehs* and *ammehs* over there. All of them loved me, and when you were taken away from me, then came back—sick with your feet swollen and unable to walk—they entertained me, telling me stories and making me small toys like that doll. Do you remember that doll? I liked it very much even though it wasn't pretty. I don't know what

78

happened to that doll. I lost it when I was in Evin. Actually, I didn't lose it. The guards took it from me. But why? It was a little doll, not very pretty, not like those I had at home. She had only two dots for eyes and some loose black threads on her head for hair. Whenever the guards came for you, I started to cry, but the *khalehs* and *ammehs* kept me occupied with that doll and told me stories about her.

Now just Grandma tells me stories. She says they are the same stories she told you when you were the same age as me. I love Grandma but I don't like that she calls me "poor child." I tell her, I'm not poor, my father and mother are engineers. She still calls me "my poor child." Nobody calls me "my daughter" anymore. I envy Lili. Do you remember Lili? But I know that you didn't see her. She was born when we were in Evin. She's Khalehs Ladan's daughter, still just a baby. She's so cute, and Khaleh Ladan calls her "my daughter," "my darling." I ask her what about me? Whose daughter am I now? She hugs me and says, "You are a courageous girl, like your maman." I want to be like you, but I don't want to be in Evin, to be flogged, have swollen and black feet, and then to go paradise. I don't want to leave my little girl without a maman and a baba. Sometimes I envy Lili, even though she's just a baby; she has a maman and a baba and I have neither.

Still, I'm wondering what happened to you. It's hard for me to believe that you left me behind and went to paradise. After you sent me home with Grandma, I never saw you again. I asked Grandma many times to take me to Evin to see you and be with you. She cried, "Damn Evin. My daughter is not there anymore."

"Where's she now?" I asked.

"She's in paradise, my poor child," she wailed. "She's among the stars." But where's paradise, for God's sake? Why won't anyone take me to paradise to be with you and Baba jaan? I miss both of you. I miss our apartment, too. You remember I had a room for myself: a bed, a dresser, and a desk. I had beautiful dolls, many toys and books. I ask Grandma to take me to our apartment. I want to sleep in my bed. Sometimes I think you and Baba jaan are there and sent me to visit with Grandma for just a few days; that you will come back and get me. But sometimes I can't remember Baba jaan's face. When I see Lili's baba, I mean Mr. Shapoor, I remember that I once had a baba too. But what happened to him? When Ammeh Pooran took me to Khanum jaan's place, I looked for my Baba jaan, but he wasn't there, either. I remember the days we went there with you and Baba jaan, and Khanum jaan always made me cookies, which I liked very much. Baba jaan made me a swing that hung from a big tree. He sat me on the swing and pushed it. Khanum jaan warned Baba jaan, "Be careful. Don't let my little girl fall or get hurt." We were so happy in those times. You and Baba jaan loved me. Whenever you picked me up from daycare, you kissed me and called me "my dear daughter." Now nobody calls me "my daughter" anymore, as if I am no one's daughter any longer. Grandma calls me "poor child." If you and Baba jaan hadn't gone to paradise or if you'd taken me with you, nobody would call me poor.

One day, when I was crying and asking for you, Grandma called me "poor child" again. I got so angry with her, I banged my head against the wall and screamed, "I don't like to be called poor! I am not poor."

She hugged me and caressed me, and said, "I know you're not poor but..."

But what? I don't understand. If I am not poor, why does Grandma call me that?

You know Maman jaan, even though I am in Grade Two, there are things I don't understand. First, why did you leave for paradise without me? Am I not your adorable daughter anymore? Is paradise a better place than our apartment? Still, I can't believe that you forgot about me. You loved me so much. I remember when we were in Evin, you hugged me so tight sometimes I couldn't breathe. Well, I didn't say anything, but I liked it. I wish those days had never ended and that I was with you all the time. I don't know what happened that you sent me home with Grandma. Your eyes were full of tears but you didn't cry. You told me, be a good girl, a courageous girl. I asked you, when are you getting out of Evin? When can I be with you again? You said nothing. I started to cry, but you hugged me and said, "You shouldn't cry. Never cry. Be a brave girl." Maman jaan, I don't know if I'm brave or not, but I know I miss you terribly.

I remember you always kissed my hands or feet when I got hurt. I wanted to do the same when your feet were swollen and black but you wouldn't let me. Why? I regret it so much that I didn't kiss your wounded feet.

You know, my Maman jaan, since you've left, the worst thing for me is going to school. I don't want to talk about it, but, well, it's hard to keep it to myself. Grandma takes me to school every day and when the kids see me with her, they ask me, "Is she your Maman?" I say, "No, she is my Grandma." Then they ask me, "Where's your maman and baba? Why don't they take you to school? Are they dead?" I scream at them and shout, "No, they're not dead! They are in paradise!"

Once, our teacher saw me crying and hitting my head with my fists. She called me and asked me what happened. I told her everything about you and Baba jaan. I even told her that I was in Evin with you and told her I don't know what happened to you and Baba jaan. Then I told her that I don't know if you're in paradise or in Beheshte Zahra. She hugged me and caressed me and said, "You are a courageous girl, like your maman. You should be proud of your maman and baba. They have been brave people."

I asked her, "Are they really in paradise? And why didn't they take me with them?"

She said, "They left you behind to continue their lives." I didn't understand her very well, but her words soothed me. She changed my seat to the front row and every once a while she smiles at me. Since then my classmates don't ask me about you and Baba jaan any more. But I don't like to be friends with them. All of them have a maman and a baba and I don't have either one. Some of them come to school in a car, but Grandma doesn't have a car. She even doesn't know how to drive. Sometimes Khaleh Ladan gives us a ride to Beheshte Zahra, but mostly we get there by bus and it makes me so tired.

Maman jaan, to tell you the truth, I don't like to go to Beheshte Zahra. I don't see you and Baba jaan there, only your names on a piece of stone. And there's nothing for me to play with, not even a swing, and if there were, who would push me?

You see Maman jaan, since you and Baba jaan left me behind and went I don't know where, I am so miserable. If Grandma calls me poor, she might be right. But I don't want to be poor. I want to be your little daughter, your adorable child, as you used to call me, to be a courageous girl. Please come back to me. I don't want you to be among the stars. There're so many stars in the sky. I want you to be here, a star with me as you were before going to Evin. I want you back, you and Baba jaan. Please, please, please.

Coffee Cup Fortune

—⟐—

A FTER FATHER CLAIMED BANKRUPTCY and sold our Niavaran house to pay his debts, Maman finally decided to pay a visit to Soraya joon. We had moved to the apartment on Mirdamad Street and our life of luxury had become a story that belonged to the past. I believed Maman wanted to reconcile with Soraya joon. It was almost two years since Soraya joon had stopped visiting us. It was my mother who had cut the string between them, which had been very strong and went back to their childhood.

A few months after buying the Niavaran house, Maman purchased a lamb and hired a butcher to behead it in the yard—to blind the jealous eyes, as folk say. Then she invited all her friends and relatives for Hazrat Abbass Sofreh, and hired a female preacher. For all these religious ceremonies and feasts, Soraya joon was present, too. As Maman used to say, she was a big help, like a real sister. We considered her our aunt, and she really was. Our only true aunt, Maman's sister, had moved to America with her family after the revolution.

When Maman and Soraya joon got together they told us about their friendship, which went back many years. They were neighbours for a while and had attended the same elementary school. After my grandfather bought his house on Mirdamad Street, Soraya joon and Maman no longer lived close to each other, but they kept in touch by phone and at various parties and events hosted by mutual friends. As Maman used to say, the similarities between them were amazing: "Soraya had one sister; me, too. I've got two daughters; Soraya, too." They don't have any physical similarities. Soraya joon is tall, slim, with black eyes, black hair, and an olive complexion. My mother is rather short and plump, always worrying about her weight, with curly, brown hair, and a light complexion. Unlike my mother, who's noisy and talkative, Soraya joon is taciturn and reserved, but a genuinely kind person. Maman always said Soraya joon wasn't so reserved and quiet when they were in high school. Soraya joon participated in almost all the school's programs, and with her nice, soft voice, she could imitate most of the famous singers, making for good times during recess.

Whenever Soraya joon came to visit—usually with her daughters, Paria and Nazli—we would sit together in the kitchen. Maman made us coffee and after we finished drinking it, Soraya joon told our fortune from our cups the way her Armenian neighbour had taught her.

Maman said, "Our real friendship started in Anooshirvan Dadgar high school in grade ten. In those days, we sometimes stayed overnight at each other's house. Our parents, too, started to develop a close friendship. We travelled together a few times, once to the Caspian seashore, and once to Isfehan and Shiraz. Those trips, I'll never forget."

Maman said, "Soraya joon's husband was the son of a friend of my grandfather. They met each other at my birthday party." At that time Soraya joon was a second-year student at the university, studying literature to be a high school teacher. My Maman hadn't been accepted at the university. As she said, she hadn't been a very good student. She was in love with her cousin—I mean, my father. Their parents weren't opposed; they wanted them to get married, and believed in the folk saying that, "A marriage between two cousins has been signed in heaven." Baba had gone to America for his education. As he later joked, travelling to America wasn't as a big deal in those days as it was after the revolution, when it was accessible only to Prophet Solomon, flying on his rug.

My father said that getting admitted to an American university was easier than being accepted in a university in Iran, where only very talented students pass the entrance exams. To attend an American university, all you needed was a high school diploma and a bank account with a considerable amount of money, which my grandfather had been able to provide.

Uncle Goodarz was studying chemical engineering in the technical faculty of Tehran University when he met Soraya joon. A few months later they became engaged but they didn't marry until they both finished their education. That year my Maman's fiancé, I mean my Baba, had retuned from the U.S. for his summer holidays. My mother and father got married and then left for America together. Two years later, my father's education was completed and they returned to Iran with Taraneh, who was six months old. Soraya joon was eight months' pregnant with Paria. So Taraneh and Paria were born in the same year, only a few months apart. Naturally, they grew up together and developed a close friendship—like Maman and Soraya joon. Sometimes, I envied them. They would close the door of Taraneh's room and not let Nazli and me in. I was sure they were talking about their boyfriends. Nazli and I weren't very intimate. She's two years older than me and never showed any interest in being my friend. She called me a mommy-daddy spoiled baby, I think because I had a room to myself and a closet full of clothes, as well as many toys and games, a guitar and a piano. Nazli and Paria had a small bedroom. Their house and ours weren't comparable. But Baba always advised us not to pay attention to what people own but how kind and good-hearted they are. "Try to value your friendships," he always said.

Uncle Goodarz was hired by the Tolidaroo Company after graduating as a chemical engineer and later they bought a little house in Bahar Street, when Paria and Nazli were still very young. Soraya joon didn't want to be far from her parents, who lived in the same area. Her mother wasn't very healthy and Soraya joon visited her every day. Soraya joon's younger sister, Zohreh, had gone to Germany, like many Iranians who fled the country after the revolution, those who had political involvements or those who couldn't stand the religious government interfering in their private lives. We wanted to leave the country, too, Maman particularly. When Taraneh and I had to wear those black *maghnehes* and dark school uniforms, Maman looked at us distressed, as if she were sending us to a torture chamber. The worst time was during the Iran-Iraq war, when Tehran was under missile attack. Maman urged Baba to arrange for us to leave Iran. Once or twice we went to the north, to our villa at the Caspian seashore. Once, Soraya joon's family visited us, but they stayed only two nights. Our villa was crowded with Baba's brother's family and our grandparents as well. My mother nagged my father to sell his properties and get a visa for America, where my aunt, her husband, and their son and daughter were living. They sent us letter after letter, writing, "Why are you staying?" Baba didn't want to leave. "Nowhere else would be like home," he used to say.

When I became older, having to be veiled was like a curse to me. Taraneh and I dreamed about leaving Iran, especially when we received photos from our cousins with their friends, boys and girls, at school or at parties, wearing tight jeans, mini-skirts, short-sleeved shirts, and colourful dresses, their hair waving in wind. They looked as happy as we imagined they would be; we thought they lived in paradise. At that time in Iran, we hardly dared to have a birthday party or listen to music that we liked, and if we did, Maman had to stand by the window to watch the street. If she noticed anything suspicious, we had to turn off the lights and music, trembling with fear that there might be a raid on our home and we would be taken to Committee for flogging. In spite of all our precautions, Taraneh and I had been taken to Committee several times because of attending birthday parties and being careless with our hijabs. And if it wasn't for Baba paying big bribes, God knows what might have happened to us.

Yes, in those days, Maman, Taraneh, and I begged Baba to send us to America. When Grandma heard us, she was angry with Maman: "Parvaneh, are you crazy? Leaving your home and going to a foreign, faraway land? Well, Farzaneh had no choice because of her husband—a shah's colonel. If he didn't leave, he would have been executed by now."

Grandpa also showered Maman with fatherly advice: "I can't believe you want to leave your old parents and go to another part of world. What's wrong with your life here or with your daughters' lives? So, the girls have to wear a veil. This is not just for your daughters—it's the same for half of the population of this country." He told Maman that if she left the country, he wouldn't call her his daughter anymore.

We lived in fear of being arrested and imprisoned. Prison meant flogging, torture, or execution, and still does. Whenever we were invited to a birthday party, Maman always accompanied us there, then talked to the hostess, giving her advice, inspecting the neighbourhood carefully, asking about possible escape routes in case there was a *pasdars* raid. When she was sure that the host and hostess were watchful, she would leave but she called us every half an hour to be sure we were safe and secure. Almost all of our friends' parents did the same. They were all afraid that something bad might happen to us.

We'd newly moved to our Niavaran house and Maman was busy with decorating and buying new furniture when Taraneh became sick. Our new house looked like a mansion, according to my friends. No one had a pool then, and if they did, they didn't dare have water in it. We had a deep well in our yard, so we could fill the pool with no need to use the city water.

Taraneh had headaches once in a while, but our parents didn't take them seriously. Then they got worse, and some days she couldn't leave her bed. My parents took her to visit every specialist they could find, but none of them could do anything for her. When she was all right for a few days, joy came back to our house, but it didn't last too long. Another severe headache would capture her and Taraneh would collapse in bed.

Grandma blamed Maman. "It's from too much work, too many classes—draining your children's energy. You don't let them enjoy their childhood, or their teenage years: piano class, mathematics class, English class, dance class, swimming class, and this and that class. When a girl gets her high school diploma, she has to marry a nice, wealthy man. Thank God your daughters won't need such wealthy men. Their father can give them enough. They need a loyal, obedient husband like their own father." Then with the same note of accusation in her voice, she asked Maman, "What's wrong with your life? You didn't have to take all those classes."

Defiantly Maman said, "My mother blames me for everything. She puts the guilt on my shoulders. I did what a mother does these days for her daughters. Many of my friends have hired a piano teacher for their children, and I did too. Is it my fault that Taraneh loves to sit at the piano and practice the melodies of Beethoven, Mozart, and I don't know who else for long hours? Well, she loves classical music. Her teacher says she has a great talent for music. She wanted to learn the setar, too. I didn't force her to do so. Now that the daughters of any grocery store owner go to university, why should my daughters end up with just a high school diploma? Why should Paria be accepted at the medical school and my Taraneh...?"

She couldn't continue after she mentioned Taraneh's name and started to cry. Taraneh hadn't taken the university entrance exams because she was sick. Baba said he'd send her to America. Taraneh said, "Who wants to go to America?" She locked herself in her room and no one dared knock on her door to ask her how she was. When Soraya joon came to visit, she knocked lightly on the door, speaking lovingly, and trying to get Taraneh to come out. If Paria was with her, Taraneh would be happier and the two of them would spend some time together in her room. Maman thanked Soraya joon, saying, "You might help her to get well."

"You should give her time," Soraya joon soothed Maman. "She might be tired, or bored, or upset…"

"Why can't the doctors figure out what's wrong with her?" Maman lamented. "If her headaches would just let her alone…"

Apparently, the doctors thought nothing was wrong with Taraneh, that she looked healthy. Still, she had lost weight. Some days, when she had a headache, she couldn't eat. On those days, our home looked like a place of mourning.

Two years passed, then three, and nothing changed. We'd already moved to our new house when Baba made an appointment with a very famous hospital in England and we went to London. It was in the summer time so I could go with them. But I didn't like London and counted the days until we could come back. We spent the whole time either sitting by Taraneh's bed in the hospital or at the hotel. Maman kept saying, "I want to leave this place as soon as possible." She couldn't speak English—she'd forgotten the little she had learned during the years they had lived in America. Baba and I interpreted the doctors' words for her and Taraneh understood even better than Baba. Finally, the doctors called Maman and Baba and in front of Taraneh told them that their examinations and tests had gone nowhere, and that they were unable to find anything wrong with Miss Taraneh. They told my parents that Taraneh might get well as time went on and she got older.

We were so happy that we flew back to Iran few days later. Then Baba insisted we go to the south of France for a week, to rest and relax after the stressful time in London. He was so happy about the doctors' opinion that he believed all of us needed some happy times. But three of us didn't want to go. I'd missed my friends and our beautiful house. Taraneh wanted to go home, too. I knew her real motive for wanting to go back to Iran right away. She missed Bijan, for sure. Nobody except

Paria, Nazli, and I knew about Bijan. If Maman and Baba found out about him, they would have made Bijan's family miserable. Taraneh had been pledged to marry her cousin, Nima, since she was born—like my parents. Nima had studied engineering at Azad University and worked in Baba's office. Their company had built a high-rise apartment building and a penthouse in the building belonged to Nima and Taraneh. But since Taraneh had become sick, no one dared mention Nima in front of her. Nima didn't come to visit her any more. He did a few times and Taraneh had made such a fuss and screamed so loudly, that Maman and Baba imagined she had become psychotic. I found out about Bijan when Taraneh started learning to play the setar. Bijan was her instructor. He was a slim, bearded young boy who had lost his father in the revolution. He lived with his mother. His only sister had left Iran to seek asylum in France. For a while, Bijan came to our house to teach Taraneh, then he stopped coming. Taraneh's illness became worse, and recurring severe headaches forced her to stay in bed. One day she told me about her love for Bijan and made me swear to God to say nothing to Maman and Baba. I became a messenger between them and kept Taraneh's secret to myself. I didn't feel it was necessary to talk about it to Maman and Baba. Taraneh and Bijan believed their love for each other was a Platonic love. When Taraneh played the setar, it was as though she was talking to Bijan, and it brought tears to my eyes. It never crossed my mind that Taraneh might one day be gone.

If Maman or Baba had thought the marriage of Taraneh and Bijan would bring back Taraneh's health, they might have beseeched him to marry her. Now I feel guilty. I wish I had told them about the couple as they might have done something. It might have saved Taraneh's life, or, at the very least, she would have had the man she loved beside her at her death bed.

Maman tried everything she could to bring back Taraneh's health. When the doctors in Iran and England weren't able to help, she went to fortune-tellers and spent lots of money on them, hoping they could tell her of something that might cure her.

When Soraya joon, Uncle Goodarz, Paria, and Nazli stopped to coming to visit, Maman didn't say anything about it. Whenever Taraneh or I asked about Soraya joon, Maman said, "She lives faraway and she is busy with her mother who is sick at home and needs someone to care for her. We shouldn't oblige them to come to visit us."

Baba's bankruptcy happened after Taraneh's death, but actually his fortunes had started to decline a few months before that. Suddenly everything turned upside down and our luxurious lifestyle vanished as if it had never existed.

Soraya joon didn't show up for Taraneh's memorial, either. It was a week or two later that I called their home to talk to Nazli. We chatted for a while and I asked about Paria. She said Paria was living in a small town in the north of Iran where she was doing her medical training. I couldn't help myself and started to cry. When she asked why I was crying, I told her about Taraneh's death. A few days later, Paria and Nazli came to visit. Maman stayed in her room; Grandma was looking after her. Paria and Nazli visited with me for about half an hour and then left.

A year or so after Taraneh's death, Maman told us about her dream: that she had seen Taraneh, who told her she missed Paria. With a sense of regret in her voice, Maman said, "Actually, it was the Niavaran house that distanced us."

I don't know what exactly happened that made Soraya joon stop visiting and what Maman said to her that brought her back to us. Soraya joon told us the whole story when she came to visit.

*

It was a Friday morning and I had slept longer than usual. When I woke up, I heard voices coming from the living room.

I knew that a few days before, Maman had gone to see Soraya joon and had asked her to come to visit.

I washed, combed my hair and changed my dress, then went to the living room to greet them. Uncle Goodarz, Paria, and Nazli were there, too. A feeling of joy and excitement momentarily warmed me and I felt as though I had returned to those happy days we'd had together. But after Taraneh's death, happiness meant nothing and returning to the past was an illusion. Not only had our wealth disappeared, but we had lost Taraneh too.

Soraya joon said, "It's good that Ghazal is here too. I have to say everything in front of you all, so there's no misunderstanding. In the past two years, Goodarz, Paria, and Nazli asked me what happened that I ended my relationship with my old friend—a friend closer to me than my own sister. What causes you to forget a forty-year friendship and to not want to mention your old and once dear friend's name? I'll tell you what happened." She looked at Maman, then at Baba and me, and continued. "Parvaneh said that a fortune teller had told her I was jealous of you after you bought your Niavaran house and that I'd cursed you. She told me that the fortune teller said I had a devil eye, and that it was the reason for Taraneh's sickness. Parvaneh told me if I stopped visiting, Taraneh would get well."

Maman was looking down at the floor, wiping tears off of her face. I imagined they were tears of shame, not for losing Taraneh. Baba didn't say a word. Since he'd had to sell the Niavaran house to pay his debts and had bought this small apartment in Mirdamad, close to Grandpa's place, he wasn't the same man any more. Losing Taraneh was a huge loss for him, too.

The whole time Soraya joon talked, we were as silent as the dead. She started to speak again, breaking the silence. This time she didn't speak about the fortune teller and what Maman had told her; instead, she talked about the past we all shared, and about the present. She told us that she was going to retire, and that her sister was going to come to visit in summer time after so many years, about her mother who wasn't in good health. She talked about many trivial things. No one else opened their mouth to say anything—it was as if we were all mute. Maman still had her head down, even though her tears had stopped running. I thought of serving them something, tea or coffee, but I was rooted to my spot on the sofa, mesmerized by Soraya joon's voice, and it seemed to me that the past was present and that Taraneh was still with us—in the kitchen, perhaps, brewing coffee. I shook my shoulders slightly and got up, but then I saw Taraneh enter the room with a tray full of cups of coffee. She moved like a ghost around the room, wearing a long white dress, like her shroud, offering each of us a cup. Then she sat beside Soraya joon, sipped her coffee, then handed her the empty cup and said, "Soraya joon, will you please tell me my fortune?"

Things were exactly like they had been in the past. Whenever Soraya joon came to visit, she made coffee for us, and we would sit around the kitchen table, laughing and chatting and sipping from our cups. When we finished, Soraya joon would read our fortune from our cups. The first thing she used to say about Taraneh's and my fortune was: "You two, well, you will both live a long life—eighty or ninety years or more."

If You Were I

—ɱ—

If he were I, he would do what I did.

—Sylvia Plath

I WAS CROSSING THE Fairview Mall food court when I saw Anna sitting on one of the padded benches. There was a small table in front of the bench, and usually there would be a single chair on the other side of the table. Really, I didn't see her, she saw me. I was several tables away from her when she called out my name. I turned and smiled at her. She waved for me to come and sit by her side. I smiled and decided to make my way over and say hello.

Anna and I have known each other for a long time. We are among those immigrants, or I should say refugees, who know each other very well, and know about the bad and good of our lives. Anna used to write short stories when she was a newcomer but she doesn't anymore, or if she does, she doesn't send them, as she used to, to the various the Iranian publications. She only feels sorry for herself.

She says she writes, but no one notices her writing and nobody reads it. Sometimes she reads her stories out loud to me and then says, "You see, it doesn't work."

When I see her sad face, I feel sorry for her and I want say, "So, why do you write? If it makes you unhappy, don't do it and be happy." But I know if I say this, it will seem as though I have cursed her; that I have implied she doesn't have any talent and doesn't have anything to say. When she gives me her writing to read, I don't say anything to her because I am not an expert in commenting on short stories or on any piece of literary work.

When we first got to know each other and both of us were newly arrived in this country, she often gave me her work to read. I had told her that I had read only a few books. When she asked me my opinion of her work, I didn't know what to say. Actually, I didn't have an opinion. I mean, no one had ever asked my opinion before. And I didn't have any comments to make about the few books that I had read. And frankly, I didn't know that a reader *could* make comments on a writer's work. I thought that writers and artists work to please themselves.

Anna always said to me, "Damn my heart! Writing has prevented me from doing anything useful. I have gotten nowhere with this writing."

I would look at her and not know what to say. I couldn't say, "So, if that's how you feel, forget about writing." I was sure that if I had told her that, she would have been devastated.

I was fully aware that writing played a big role in her life. She had been a writer in Iran, and had published a collection of stories. She said, "It was the beginning of my career. I had just started to write and I had a collection of short stories published, but the book didn't get any reviews. Don't think that I was looking for a name or for fame." I looked at her and said nothing. She must have realized that my knowledge of literature was meager. I have never worked outside the house and, as I said, I haven't read many books. I have raised four children.

Anna used to say, "You're lucky because you weren't forced to work in this country." Anna works in a big laundry, though she never talks about what she does there, and I haven't asked her, either. For a while, she had a lot of pain in her arm and she stayed home; she was covered by workers' compensation, although she was expected to return to her job in less than a year. She said, "I wish I could retire, but I still have ten or more years ahead of me."

I tell her that when she's retired, she can work full-time on her writing. She looks at me dumbfounded and says nothing.

When I get to Anna's table, I don't see the chair that is usually there. She tells me to grab a nearby chair and sit down. I do, even though I don't have too much time. I have to be at home in an hour to make dinner for Hamed.

Anna says, "You're one of those happy immigrants." There's no jealousy in her words.

I say, "God has mercy on me, but not on Hamed. I have to carry the burden of his pain as well. Do you think that's happiness?"

She says, "You're right."

I say, "In Iran, Hamed was the manager of a big company and he had more than five hundred people were working for him, and here…"

She interrupts, "It doesn't matter."

I say, "Everyone here is trained for a special job. Hamed is not made for this job he's doing here."

This dialogue between us never reaches a satisfactory conclusion. I lean forward in my chair to face her directly and ask, "Why are you so upset?"

She says, "Upset? How did you know?"

"I can tell by the look on your face. You started writing something?"

"I wanted to write but…"

I know that Anna is once again trapped in what she usually calls *writing blindness*. She believes the words are not there anymore—that she cannot see them. Then she says, "There's another problem, though, " and pauses, as if to reassure herself that I'm waiting to hear more.

I ask her, "What is it then?"

She says, "You know that it's been a while since I left aside writing, but I read. Reading gives me peace. I feel free and I can

get away from my situation here and travel to new worlds."
When she mentions travel, I feel sad. I know how much she loves to travel, but she can't. I've just come back from Los Angeles; we went to visit one of Hamed's aunts. We took a trip to San Francisco by train as well. When I had talked to her about my trip, I noticed immediately envy and pain in her eyes, so I stopped. She had said, "Tell me everything. Don't cut your story short. Tell me what you've seen. I can dream about what you tell me and imagine myself in your place."

Today, there's a new sadness in her face, a pain like a wound that is not old yet. An old wound has a special colour, but a new one darkens the face. I look at her, but she steals her eyes away from me and says, "Don't look at me that way. I'm not a good person."

Surprised, I say, "What do you mean? Are you crazy?"

She says, "I came here to feel the vastness."

I laugh and say, "Here? Vastness? Here is suffocating."

She says, "My apartment is what's suffocating."

"Your home is beautiful," I say.

"What kind of beauty does a thirty-square-metre apartment have? I am suffocating there," she says.

I say, "But it's yours—you own it. You have spent money on it, money that came from your hard work and your sweat. You've decorated it beautifully, like a garden. It looks like an art gallery."

I try to remember the word in Farsi for art gallery, but I can't. Whenever I use English words instead of Farsi, Anna always finds the Farsi word and corrects me, but this time she says nothing. I can see that she's sad.

She says, "I'm the slave to a thirty-square-metre apartment and you think of it as my little garden or my art gallery?"

I say, "We are all slaves. Aren't we? Isn't Hamed a slave as well? Hamed is a slave of one-thousand-square-metres and you are a slave of thirty-square-metres."

She puts her hand up and says, "Enough philosophizing."

"Tell me why you are so upset?" I say, gently. "You have never been so sad. You are usually the epitome of joy, work, and effort. Maybe I can help."

She says, "My conscience hurts me. Today I did something against my conscience and now I feel I don't have a conscience."

I look at my watch and at the people who are sitting around us. I don't have more than half an hour. I look at a man sitting beside us. He is scratching a lottery card with a coin. He hopes to win a big chunk of money. And I imagine that right now, in his dreams, he is flying over the clouds.

Anna asks, "Are you listening to me? I have to confess. I have to talk about the sin I committed today."

"Sin?" I repeat. "Do you believe in sin?"

"I've always believed in sin," she says.

I say, "Well, tell me."

She doesn't look at me, doesn't want to see in my eyes what I might be thinking about her at this moment. She looks this way and that way, at the food booths, of which there are many, at the two Chinese women sitting beside us who are talking non-stop, at a man who has a bunch of lottery tickets and is erasing the numbers with a coin; it seems he hasn't won anything yet. She looks farther away, where people are coming and going.

Anna says, "It happened today, less than an half an hour ago. I came here to feel vastness. I couldn't walk outside; it was cold, it was cloudy, snow was forecast. There was nowhere to go except here. I didn't want to eat something or even have a cup of coffee. I didn't have money to spend, nor an appetite for anything to eat or drink. You know that I have to stop myself from these kinds of luxuries, so as to be able to pay my mortgage. And God only knows how many more years it will take before my little garden truly will be mine."

She laughs but I don't. I see her sad face, and can't smile. I just look at her and wait for her to finish.

She continues, "So, I chose this cozy corner and sat. I had brought my notebook to write in, just randomly. I mean, to jot down whatever came to my mind. Just for myself. Then a person who wasn't exactly like a person, either—I suppose he was a little sad, or maybe even devastated—he stood in front of me and wanted to sit in the chair you are sitting in now. I said, my friend has gone to get a coffee.... I looked up at him and saw my own reflection in his eyes. He looked shattered. Then the man left. I got up, took the chair, and placed it at the next table. A few minutes later, the man came back. He looked at me, noticed the chair was gone, and said, "Your friend...?"

I said nothing. He realized that I didn't want him sitting in front of me. I watched him as he walked around the food court. He couldn't find anywhere else to sit. Nobody wanted him to sit at their table. He left and I said nothing. Then I asked myself, "What happened to my conscience? Where has it gone? Do I really have a conscience? Wouldn't it have been better to have stayed in my own apartment and not look for vastness?"

I nod but say nothing.

She says, "Is it selfishness or lack conscience?"

I say nothing.

She says, "I know that to judge is difficult."

I say, "Yes, to judge is difficult."

*

After supper I tell Anna's story to Hamed. He says nothing. I ask him, "What can be done?"

He asks, "What do you mean by that?"

I say, "Do you think Anna is a person without a conscience?"

"What a question! How do I know? Am I to judge Anna's conscience?"

"If you were in her place, would you have given a seat to that person?"

He says, "If you knew how exhausted I am and what a dirty day I've had, you wouldn't be asking me these silly questions."

He gets up, leaves the living room, and goes into the washroom, then turns on the faucets so he can't hear me if I say something.

*

A week goes by and I don't see Anna or hear from her, but I think about her and that man with his unpleasant appearance, as if it was I who hadn't give him a place to sit. After a week I call her to ask how she is.

She says, "What has happened that you are asking about me?"

I say, "I always ask how you are."

She says, "You probably want to know what I did with my conscience and how I got rid of the torture."

I ask, "How?"

She says, "So, you still remember our conversation?"

I say, "Yes, I remember it."

She says, "I see him in my dream and I dance with him. We don't hate each other any more. I mean, I don't hate him. I tell him I'll always keep a seat for him and he has promised to get a coffee for me. He says he usually has enough money to pay for one or two cups of coffee. He says he's not worried about mortgage or rent. He sleeps wherever he finds a place, and during the days..."

I continue, "He keeps looking for an empty seat."

Anna says, "I hope he doesn't run into anyone like me."

I ask her, "Have you seen him again?"

She says, "I told you already. He appears in my dream and dances with me."

Snake

—⟋⟍—

SORAYA SAYS, "Dr. Doostar is sick."

"Sick?" I say, surprised. "I don't think he's sick. Yes, he's old. It might be his age—late eighties—that has affected him and perhaps he doesn't look as well as he used to. But he certainly is not sick."

We were invited to Dr. Farhoodi's place to celebrate Yalda. Dr. Farhoodi is a physician who's now retired. We were about eight people. The youngest of our group was past fifty, so we were all of a certain age. Our children were grown up and had their own lives. And as folks say, all of us had experienced both bad and good in our lives.

It was after midnight and we were almost done discussing politics, literature, society, the Iranian community, education, family matters, and anything else that came to our minds, especially our health problems, which currently tend to dominate our conversations. A visible fatigue had spread over our faces. I don't know how our talk turned to dreaming and its connection to real life. Hamid, Soraya's husband, who had studied psychology when he was young and was now writing articles about the subject for Iranian newspapers in the city, said, "Dreams in many ways have some connection to the individual's consciousness."

Akbar, who is a chartered accountant and works at a well-known company, didn't agree with Hamid. He argued that dreams had nothing to do with real life and that they only relate to the individual's unconscious. The discourse between the two was becoming heated; no one else could get a word in.

When Hamid mentioned Carl Jung, the famous psychologist, Dr. Doostar coughed loudly and everyone turned toward him. The entire night he hadn't uttered more than a few words; he had thanked Dr. Farhoodi's wife, our hostess, and made a few casual and flattering remarks. His silence was unusual, because at many other gatherings he had always been talkative and witty.

By the time the Dr. Doostar's coughing fit had ended, Akbar and Hamid had forgotten about their disagreement. Dr. Doostar cleared his throat and with his coarse voice, which sounded like banging on a rusty pot, said, "Do you want to hear a real story?" as if he was addressing a group of his medical students. Dr. Doostar told us that he had been a university professor in Iran, but it was hard to believe him because he didn't seem to have a medical specialty. Without giving us a chance to respond, he continued, "It's a story that when you hear it, for sure you will say, 'It cannot be true.' Or 'It was a dream or an illusion.' But the fact is that this story is true and and it really happened to me. For years I forced myself to believe that what had happened to me had been a dream, to help me to deal with it and not go mad. But my story..." and here he paused for a moment. "I don't know why I call it a story. The word 'story' diminishes the reality of my memory. Yes, I have to say that what happened to me was pure fact. After you hear it, I leave it to you to believe it or not, to think of it as a dream or as reality..."

The doctor's preamble took so long that Dr. Farhoodi permitted himself to interrupt him, "Dear Doctor, you're making us impatient. Please don't fly from one subject to another. We are..."

Dr. Doostar obviously didn't hear Dr. Farharoodi because he simply continued, "First of all, promise that you won't interrupt me. It's true that I'm old and sometimes I mix things up and become forgetful, but the story that I'm going to tell you is one of those…"

Again, he didn't finish and instead looked blankly at us. It seemed that he didn't notice us. His expression was distant and his eyes were searching beyond us. He said, "No, I shouldn't call it a story. But in some ways it sounds like fiction. Yes, it has crossed my mind many times that I could turn this experience into a story. If Sadegh Hedayat were alive, he might have written a fantastic novel based on this story."

Dr. Farhoodi's wife interrupted him again and said, "Minoo is a writer, too." She was referring to me.

To show my humility, I wanted to say, *no, I am not a writer yet,* but Dr. Doostar, without troubling to look at me, as if I didn't exist as a writer or even as a human being, said, "No." His "no" was so forceful that he made me believe I'd never be a writer.

Dr. Doostar, with the same forceful tone, which did not match his wrinkled complexion and crumpled body, said, "Only Sadegh Hedayat could write a novel about what I'm going to tell you."

Dr. Farhoodi was getting ready to say something again when Dr. Doostar turned to look at him directly and said, "If you could be a little patient…"

Then, for the first time he focused his gaze on all of us as if he wanted to be sure of our presence. He said, "Please, just listen for fifteen minutes."

We assured him we were listening to his story with all of our attention.

Dr. Doostar cleared his throat and finally started his story.

"I had just become a physician and had started a practice in a small town that was even smaller than my birthplace. I had an office and I dreamt of being famous and rich, which was my motivation for studying medicine in the first place. I even worked till late at night to treat one or two more patients so I could earn more money. I had nothing to do at home anyway. In those days, radio and television weren't available to everyone. I didn't have a radio. I didn't buy newspapers either, reluctant to spend a few coins. I had nothing to do with what was going on in the world. My world was my office and my patients, who were old and young, men and women, and children, occupied my whole time. They were mostly from villages in the surrounding areas of the town, and they sometimes couldn't afford my fee, despite the fact that my fees were low because I was a novice doctor. I wasn't the kind of person to examine a patient without charging him or her. If that had been the case, I would have opened a free clinic. When the patients didn't have money to pay my fee, I sent them home and told them to come back when they had money in their pockets. Those poor people went back to their homes without getting examined or treated. I thought, it's not my business—either they get through the winter and get well by chance, or they won't make it to the spring. I was a physician and my only income was from charging my patients. I dreamed of accumulating a large amount of wealth, and I eventually did. That's how I was able many years later to send my only child to Canada and afford to pay for him to get his specialty in brain surgery. But let us forget about these things.

"The poor peasants mostly came back because their sickness was acute and they needed treatment. Peasants don't usually see a doctor for a simple cold or a headache. They have to be really sick and feel pain to their bones before they even think about getting help from a doctor. Sometimes when their sickness was serious, they had to sell their poultry or their rations of flour for the cold days of winter to be able to pay for a visit. There was a government hospital which was free for everyone. So, I didn't feel bad if I sent them there because they couldn't pay me.

"I wasn't a social reformer and didn't even think about rescuing human beings. I didn't have any illusions. My only aim was to write prescriptions that would heal my patients, of course, but make me some money in return."

He paused briefly, then continued, "I didn't mean to talk about such trivial issues. My story is about something else."

We remained silent, now eager to hear the doctor's story.

"It was a winter night, perhaps Yalda night. In those years, I didn't care very much about celebrating Yalda and those kinds of festivities. At the time, I didn't have any family around me to remind me about them. However, it was a long and cold night, although I had light and heat in my office, but that light was a problem for me. It was about an hour since I'd dismissed my last patient and I was counting my earnings for the day. Actually, it had been a good day for me in terms of income. The fall was always the season of prosperity; not only for peasants, who were harvesting their crops, but also for me, because it was the season of colds, fevers, and diarrhea. Well, diarrhea was generally the result of eating too much junk food and catching the flu was easy with the change in weather. And peasants remembered their own chronic pains, which they didn't have a chance to think about during the spring and summer, the seasons of cultivation and harvesting. Now, let's forget about these things."

I was getting fed up with the doctor's asides. Once or twice I wanted to excuse myself and leave the room, pretending I had to go to the washroom, but I respected him and stayed quiet. Indeed, the silence in the room was solemn and heavy. We all waited for the doctor to continue.

"Yes, I remember very well that it was a long winter night and I was reviewing my account and happy that I had a good business. Don't laugh at me when I say business. Being a doctor is a certain kind of business. However, to make it short, when I raised my head, a young woman with a frightened expression on her face was standing in front of me. Her long, black hair was dishevelled and she was covering her breasts with her arms. Her cheeks were crimson, the front of her dress was open and her large breasts swelled beneath her arms with her panting. Then I remembered that I'd forgotten to lock my office door after seeing my last patient out. Believe me, for a few minutes I thought I was hallucinating. The woman didn't look real. She had dark almond eyes, long, perfectly-arched eyebrows, full lips—half-open and ready for a long kiss—rosy cheeks, and long, curly hair. She looked like one of the women in the paintings in books by the great Sufi poet, Hafiz, or in Omar Khayam's *Rubaiyat*. She was, I thought, what Sadegh Hedayat once described as the "eternal woman." She completely bewitched me. Obviously, she had run a long way and the wind had tangled her hair. She was panting hard. I assumed she had fled from someone or something. It crossed my mind that a wolf or a fox had followed her.

"I was so surprised and so stunned by her appearance that I couldn't utter a word. Yes, I remember now, she was the first to speak. Because she was still so out of breath, she stammered a little. 'My dear doctor, please help me, please. My ... my husband wants to kill me.'

"Then, I understood what was going on. Her husband, I thought, must be one of those jealous husbands and maybe someone had looked at his wife with lust in his eyes, and he had felt degraded, and then wanted to kill his wife. I wanted to say, 'Well, my dear, this is none of my business. You should complain to the police.' But the woman continued, 'My husband imagines I am a snake, a snake...'

"The word 'snake' terrified me. She pronounced it as she were a real snake, making a hissing sound as she spoke—*fesh, fesh, fesh*. There was a terrible fear in her eyes.

"I don't know if it was fear, compassion, or temptation.... Yes, I think it was temptation that forced me to get up from my desk and move toward the woman. I looked at her wide, terrified eyes and said, 'Your husband must be insane.'

"Her eyes widened further as she said, 'No, my dear doctor. He's not insane. He's a perfectly healthy man. He's the son of the village owner and bought me with a good price from my father and wants to have children by me to keep his property.'

"I asked her, 'Are you his legal wife or...?'

"She didn't let me finish. She said, 'I'm his legal wife. I am his only wife. My husband is a young man—he's only a few years older than me. But tonight, I don't know what happened to him. He said that I'd become a snake. He wanted to kill me with an axe, so I fled from him. I ran all the way from the village to the town. Then I noticed that there was a light in your office....'

"You see, it *was* the light in my office that got me into trouble. The woman bewitched me as a snake bewitches a tiny mouse. I forgot all about the oaths I'd taken as a physician and the restraints I should have exercised while examining a young woman. I had nothing left except empty words.

"I told her I'd have to examine her to determine if she was really a snake. It seemed that the woman didn't understand what I was saying. I led her to the examination table, and she yielded to me. I made love to her and she didn't resist, as if she had run all the way from her village to the town to come to my dingy office and go to bed with me. When I was done, I got off the examination table and turned my back to her so that she could dress. I waited politely for a few moments then turned around to face her. To my horror, a large snake was coiled on the examination table where she had been only moments before. It raised its head and its tongue was like a sharp blade flicking out of its mouth.

"I don't know how I got out of my office, but I fled as fast as I could and was lost in the winding alleys of the town. I must have fallen asleep outside of town at the foot of the town gates. When I awoke, it was morning. Without daring go back to my office or even to my own home to get a few pieces of my clothing, I took a bus to Tehran. I spent a few days in my parents' house, but I didn't feel well. I was plagued by visions of that woman's face, her incredible beauty, her long, lustrous hair quickly morphing into the huge, coiled snake poised and alert on the examination table. I didn't dare return to my town or go back to work in my office. One day as I was wandering idly in the streets, the headline in a newspaper attracted my attention: *A peasant killed his wife with an axe, having imagined she had turned into a snake when he was sleeping with her.*

"After reading that article, I convinced myself that what had happened to me was not real but merely a hallucination. I have never talked about it till now."

Dr. Doostar stopped talking and gazed at us with eyes full of unanswered questions. It was as if he was asking, "Now tell me: what happened to me, was it real, or not?"

Heart's Language

FOR ME, TRANSLATION IS LIKE emigration from one's homeland to another one—living in a new country and assimilating into and accepting a new way of life, uprooting everything familiar to become integrated into a foreign culture. And sometimes translation is like navigating on a sea that hasn't been charted. Translation is a captivating ordeal for me. It has been said that language is the house of the heart. When you have to move from your familiar house to another one, you can expect to confront a hard job ahead.

I have experience translating and sometimes people say, "You translate your own work, so it shouldn't be hard for you because you have the freedom to change your sentences and rewrite them so they can be translated more easily." Sometimes I do that, but my own language then loses its flavour and becomes bland. Farsi is a metaphorical language—full of expressions and proverbs that are integrated into literary language, making it very difficult to translate.

When I translated the first collection of my short stories, I gave them to a Canadian friend—my landlord, actually—to read and comment on. When she returned my writing, she had highlighted almost half of each page in bright pink marker. I felt ashamed of my poor knowledge of the English language. I wanted to submit my work to a publisher, with the expectation that it would be accepted for publication and that I would be recognized as a writer in this society.

My friend, who is also an instructor and teaches English as a second language to newcomers, looked at me the way that a doctor might look at a patient and said, "I'm sorry, but this is not English—"

I stared at her without making a sound, ashamed of my writing and deeply disillusioned. *What should I do now?* I asked myself.

She noticed my devastation and continued, "I have a suggestion."

I tried to swallow my disappointment and allowed myself to feel hopeful. "Everything will be okay," she said, a phrase I've heard on many occasions during my years of living in exile, and they had no effect on me.

But I pretended to be jubilant and asked, "What do you suggest?" And this time I really tried to feel hopeful that she could show me a magic way to perfect my English and become an expert in literary translation.

She stared at me with kindness and sympathy and said, "If you really want your writing to appear to be written by an English-speaking person, you must forget your first language and write in English—only English. You should think in English, read in English, and speak in English."

When she noticed the stupefied look on my face, she continued with sternness, "You probably know your first language always creates a barrier that interferes with learning a second language. When you are about to speak English, you think first in Farsi and then translate into English before you utter the words out loud. So your first language is always with you and it won't let you get familiar with the English language. Everyone who listens to you will recognize quickly that English is not your first language."

I was offended but I encouraged myself to respond. "I don't want anyone to imagine that English is my first language. Obviously, I am Farsi-speaking. Why should I pretend to be English-speaking? When I open my mouth to speak English it is clear that English is my second language because of my accent. I can't change my accent..."

She interrupted me, "I know. You don't need to tell me. I'm an English Language instructor. But still, if you want to be a writer with works published in English, as I said, you need to forget your first language."

I didn't want to interrupt her but her suggestion irritated me. What did she mean? Do I have forget my beloved Farsi? Stop speaking, reading, and writing in Farsi? Do I have to forget all the poems flowing in me that are in my own tongue? Is it possible? No, this wouldn't be possible for me. I couldn't empty myself of my mother tongue. That was simply beyond my strength. So I interrupted her, even though I knew it was rude. "That's impossible," I said with a deep frustration in my heart, "my mother tongue is my identity. I can't forget it."

She gently placed her hand on my shoulder and said, "I'm not saying that you must forget your mother tongue. I'm saying when you write in English, forget about Farsi. Try to write directly in English. Train your brain to write in English until you become fluent and proficient in this language. If you translate your own Farsi works, you will always be considered a translator and the language of your stories will never be genuine, or original." She then mentioned a few writers whose mother tongue wasn't English, but whose work, because it was composed in English, did not have a problem with language, diction, or expression.

"If these famous writers write in English and are successful," I comment, "then maybe it's because they learned to speak English when they were still a child in their own country, or they grew up in this country. For me, it was different. I was middle-aged when I immigrated to this country. English was a subject I was taught in high school and in college but my knowledge was limited to a few conversational sentences, such as: 'What's your name? How much does it cost?' Or, 'The weather is fine.' Or 'It's raining.' Once in this country, I didn't have the opportunity to go to college to learn English well and make it an internal language for myself. Nor did I have enough money to pay someone with perfect English to translate my Farsi fiction. In my homeland, I was a writer and I wanted to be recognized as a writer in this country as well. So the only thing I could do was translate my own work. I'm sure you think it was an ambitious task and a dream beyond my capabilities. So, it seems I should forget about it."

"You shouldn't give up your dream so quickly," she said. "I know that you're a hard worker and I've noticed that every night your light is on until late."

A cold sweat sent shivers down my spine. *God help me*, I thought. *She probably wants to increase the rent.* I looked at her with suspicion, suddenly doubting her motives. Perhaps because she knows I am awake till late, she will say that I consume more electricity than I am permitted.

But her tone was still soothing, and flipping through the pages I had given her without paying attention to any paragraph, she continued, "I remember an expression you repeat several times: 'If someone really wants something, they will get it with hard work.' So you, too, must want it."

I was still disappointed but thankful that she didn't mention increasing the rent. "How?" I asked.

"As I said, forget about your mother tongue," she said sternly, like a teacher admonishing her student.

I opened my mouth to say, *I can't, it's impossible,* but she didn't let me utter one word. "You must forget about your first language. Start to think in English, to speak in English, to read in English, and write in English. You must do it very seriously and constantly."

As I listened to her, it seemed to me I was navigating the waters of a foreign sea. I asked myself how long I would be lost on this huge ocean with no shore in sight. And, if after many years of doubting where I would land, what direction would I, could I, take?

My friend waited patiently, then asked, "What do you think?" And I, like a person standing by the shore at the beginning of this intricate and unknown journey, said, "I'm afraid to start."

"Why?" she asked, surprised.

"I'm afraid I will reach *nowhere*," I said.

"I don't understand what you mean," she said.

I realized my translation of this Farsi expression was incomprehensible in the English words I used. I said, "It's a Farsi expression and it's hard to put it into English words exactly as it is."

She laughed loudly and said, "You see, this is the first language's intrigue. You have to release yourself from the first language. You have to forget Farsi expressions and find English expressions that relay the same meaning. If you translate Farsi expressions literally, word for word, they might not make sense."

"I can't," I said. "It's not easy."

"You have to," she said with a sense of superiority in her voice.

I stayed quiet—wondering. I was disappointed and realized she could do nothing for me. She got up to leave and repeated her words once more, "Think about it. If you want to be an English language writer, you should forget..." I didn't hear the rest of her sentence. Too pungent for me to swallow. I had to find another way, but how? I didn't know.

She placed my writing—crimson with shame—on the table and left. She had been sympathetic, but she obviously didn't see a bright future for my writing in English. She held her tongue, though, and it was as if my own papers chided me: *Translation isn't easy. If you want your work to be published in English, if you want a publisher to get beyond the first manuscript pages, you must forget your mother tongue. The sweet, rhythmic Farsi that interweaves with and emerges from your flesh and bones. Forget the fairy tales you heard as a child, forget the poems of Hafiz, Rumi, Khaiam, Nima Shamloo, Sepehri, Forugh. Leave behind the community newspapers and Iranian websites in which you find beautiful poems to revive and refresh your soul.*

These thoughts made me miserable and my eyes filled with tears.

I saw my friend beside me, a ghostly voice repeating her pessimistic words, "Remember, you're living in an English-speaking country..."

I didn't hear the rest of her words. I didn't need to hear them.

I tried to follow my friend's advice. For a few months I read only books and newspapers in English and I wrote only in English. I tried to think in English too, but mostly my mind became blank, as if I had less and less to think about. It seemed as though a murky veil surrounded me, sometimes gloomy, on occasion clear, as if a lace curtain separated me from the texts I was reading.

And when I began to write in English, it got worse. The words seemed to come, not from my skin and flesh, but from somewhere unknown, where I could neither feel nor touch them. When I wanted to put an idea down on paper, the words fled from my memory, disappeared like wisps of smoke in the air, their meanings dissolving in my mind. Even when I was sure I knew the right words, had heard them on many occasions, and read them in many texts, when I tried to use them in creative writing, they seemed to play a game with me, fleeing from my mind and leaving me bewildered and frustrated. When I tried to read back my writing, the words seemed without soul or life. These words weren't mine. Fictional characters were as stiff as mannequins with blank faces. They were like unfinished sculptures that still needed a lot of work to take shape. I hardly recognized my own writing. The plot and the descriptive passages were foreign to me. A voice inside me yelled, *You're not an English-language writer. Your heart's language is Farsi; don't abandon it. Farsi, as Jamalzadeh said, is sugar.*

For me, Farsi is much better than sugar, better than anything I can imagine. When I read Rumi's poetry for the first time, my joy was compounded by the realization that I shared this great poet's mother tongue. I could read Rumi's poetry in the language in which it was written, and it could speak directly to my heart.

So, once again I took refuge in Farsi. I have chosen to continue to write in my first language and to translate it afterwards, into English. I force myself to emigrate from my own beloved homeland to a foreign one, finding my way through its winding alleys and its semi-dark hallways. And, I have to navigate seas on which I find myself afloat for the first time. Each time I reach a far shore with new earth under my feet, I reencounter the process of becoming familiar and safe. I still have a long road ahead of me, a path on which perhaps English will gradually become bright and clear as a language for writing, and then I can perhaps internalize it like my mother tongue— the language of my heart.

An earlier version of this story was published in a collection of short stories, Speaking in Tongues: Pen Canada Writers In Exile, *edited by Maggie Helwig (The Banff Centre, 2005).*

Geranium Family

—⚋—

A YOUNG CHINESE WOMAN led Sima to Farah's cubicle and asked her to be seated. Sima was taken aback when she entered the space. It was small and narrow like a coffin that not only pressed against her body but her soul as well. She remembered Farah's office in Tehran, when they worked together in the government Planning and Budget Department. That had been a spacious room with a large desk, lush green plants next to a large window, and a sofa for visitors. Sima felt as if Farah had been cheated.

She could hear the murmur of conversation and the clatter of computer keyboards coming from behind the privacy panels that served as walls. The panels were not very tall and the ceiling seemed high and far away. Sima was bewildered by the space and it seemed to her that there were many secrets behind the panels. She looked at the computer on Farah's desk—colourful images danced on its screen as if to suggest that the work was full of happiness and joy.

"You have an office?

"Yes, I do, and a boyfriend, too."

"Wow, and who is he? I didn't know you were so clever. When did you meet him?"

"The day I started to work in this department."

"Who is he then?"

"Siamak."

"Siamak? That civil engineer, the tall, handsome man? So, you are a smart girl! I envy you."

A photo of Farah, Hassan, and their two daughters was sitting on the desk. The four of them had forced smiles on their faces, showing their teeth, as if they were pretending to be happy. Sima involuntarily giggled, "The happy family." That sparked a memory of a sitcom she used to watch on television in Iran, *The Geranium Family*. For a while, it was a popular comedy that everyone in Iran watched and talked about. It was about a family that tried hard to be perfect. Sima smiled and thought she should tease Farah about this when she saw her.

"Are you really going to leave forever?" Sima asked.

"I think so. Hassan believes we have to flee as soon as possible. He says the clergy here are not giving educated people a chance. Sooner or later, we will be forced to forget our university degrees and open a grocery store."

"But it's not possible. They need us. We have knowledge, we have experience."

"Maybe they need men's knowledge, but not ours. You and I, despite our degrees in computer programming, will be forced to stay home and cook meals for our husbands, and give birth to a bunch of children."

Farah finally returned and entered the cubicle. Instead of hugging Sima, as she always did, she shook her hand formally as if she were a client. She sat on her chair, which was too big for her tiny body—her feet barely touched the floor. One of her small, plump hands rested on her desk, toying with a pen. She smiled at Sima and asked, "Tell me, how are you? Is everything okay?" There was a mischievous twinkle in her brown eyes.

Sima wanted to say not yet, but Farah didn't give her chance to respond. She turned her chair so that she faced Sima directly, looked deeply into her eyes, and said, "You must be patient. It's not as easy as you think. It was hard for us, too. It's hard for everybody." She was speaking like an authority.

"I have to find a job," Sima said in a subdued, voice. "I'm worried about Siamak. Our savings are running out." She paused, tried hard to avoid tears, and swallowed the lump in her throat. "How do I say this? I didn't imagine it like this."

Farah eyed Sima with a measure of compassion and said, "Well, when you are there, you have another image of here. But I wrote you about everything. I talked to you on the phone. I told you that this wasn't paradise."

"We didn't come looking for a paradise. We had to leave."

"So, you should get on with it. You should get on with it in any case."

"Do you think Farah can help me?" Sima asked Siamak.

"What kind of help you do expect from your friend?" Siamak answered. "I don't think she is a saint that can perform miracles."

"She's my old friend. She's been living in this country for ten years already. She may know some ways."

"What ways? Their situation was different. They came here with lots of money. They didn't have to buy dollars on the black market. They didn't have to pay a smuggler."

The telephone rang. Farah swivelled smoothly in her chair to reach for the receiver. With her profile to Sima, she spoke into the mouthpiece in a clipped tone. Her accent was unfamiliar to Sima. The expression on her face could have been surprise, indifference or anger. Sima couldn't tell. Then she hung up the phone and remained silent for a moment, not turning back to Sima.

"You finally decided to get married. Who's the lucky guy?" Sima asked.

"Not a civil engineer and not as handsome as your fiancé, but I had to choose someone. I am not as pretty as you, either, and I don't want to be like a grandmother for my children."

"Who is he, then?"

"Hassan."

"The guy in accounting department? Well, if you love him, that's enough."

"Love is not a big deal. Today's values are money and appearance."

"I hope you're not interested in only those superficial values."

Sima waited for Farah to speak. She imagined Farah might be having some problems at her work. She wanted to ask her, but she didn't. She didn't have any idea what Farah's job entailed or what responsibilities she might have. She knew she was a computer programmer in a big company. Farah had told her before that she should have been considered one of the top employees in the organization, but because she was from a Third World country, she wasn't given a promotion nor the job she really deserved.

"Am I disturbing you?" Sima asked.

Farah turned to her with a visibly reddened face. "Not at all," she said. "It's my lunch time. Nobody is allowed to interrupt me during this time. Well, that's it. Anyhow..."

"You look troubled. Is there a problem?"

"Problem? Problems never end. That's life, and I have to deal with it. Things here are no better than in large companies in Iran. Do you remember when we were employed how much they hurt us at the beginning. Not you so much because you were always an obedient, patient, and quiet person, and more than that, you were beautiful, but me.... The men couldn't bear having a woman working beside them. They wanted all women to be like their own wives, preparing them dinner, and being ready for them in the bed..." She stopped abruptly.

"Here, too?" Sima asked.

"Oh," Farah said, "how do I tell you? Here, everybody is against everybody. One has to have the skin of wolf to be able to stand it. Do you think if they give you a cubicle, like this, with a desk, a computer, and a telephone, it's over? No, my dear, it's the beginning of problems. The people who work here are of many races and nationalities. And each one wants to hire only their own friends. And Canadians want to lord it over all of them."

"What about you?" Sima asked. "Do you have any fellow countrywomen here?"

"No, I'm alone. And because of that, all the problems are on my shoulders. I wish you could get a job here. Think about it; then you and I could work together again. But you haven't been accepted as an immigrant yet, and well, there is also the language problem. All of us have language problems. This problem will never be solved, because English is not our native tongue even if we started to learn it when we were growing up. For me, language has been a barrier for so long and I'm sure it will continue to be in the future too."

"How did you get the promotion so quickly?" Farah asked. "I'm sure Siamak helped you."

"No. Siamak is going to leave the Planning and Budget Department. I got the promotion because I finished the project ahead of time. I work hard for them."

"And because you are obedient to them."

"I'm not obedient. I'm a hard worker and I'm dutiful."

Farah's hand stretched toward the telephone, and mumbling "Excuse me" to Sima, she dialled a number. She started to speak again in her Farsi-English accent. She talked slowly and clearly and sometimes she paused to search for a word, repeating, "How do I say...?"

"I can't believe you're going so far away," Sima said. "I'm sure

I'll miss you. We've been together since high school. And then in college ...how happy we were. Then working together in the Planning and Budget Deopartment. But now you're leaving me behind. I consider you my sister. I'll miss you."

"I'll miss you, too. And we can still be friends."

"No, we won't. You're going to a new country. You'll find new friends."

"Why don't you emigrate, too?"

"No, I don't want to raise my children in a foreign country. I don't want to leave my family. I'm my mother's only daughter; she wouldn't be able to bear it. Siamak doesn't like the idea of emigrating, either. He has a good job here. Consulting engineers are in demand, and we have a comfortable life here. It's not easy to start all over again."

"Maybe you're right—you have everything here. You have your mansion, you have your villa on the Caspian shore, Siamak has his private office—you can't risk everything in a new country."

"Well, how do you find Canada? Is it paradise for you?" Hassan asked, offering a glass of whiskey to Siamak and a glass of wine to Sima.

Siamak didn't reply. He glanced at Sima with a bored expression.

"We aren't looking for paradise," Sima said. "We came here because we had to. Life was becoming unbearable in Iran. We had many problems in recent years. The guards invaded our house during Maziar's birthday. Another time all our rugs and our jewellery were stolen. Mona was arrested in the street because she was walking with her boyfriend. So we had to be uprooted."

"How many times have I told you," Hassan said, "that dealing with religious people is not easy. They don't understand a single logical word. But you were optimistic, saying that they won't stay long, they'll give up. They won't give anything up.

They want to take, not to give anything to anyone. This is how they live."

Siamak remained silent. He was tired of Hassan boasting about the income from his grocery store, the cottage they had just bought on Georgian Bay.

"But nobody knew that our revolution would end like this," Sima said. "We had hope. We never imagined there would be a war after the revolution, a war for nothing, and that our children would be in danger, that the price of everything would become astronomical, that our jobs would disappear. Who could predict such a nightmare?"

"Me," Hassan said, with a clear pride. "How many times did I mention the story of Kalileh Damenh. Do you remember it?"

Siamak remembered it very well. The story was told over and over again at family gatherings. He said, "Yes, I do. And now you're the first fish, who anticipated the situation and fled before the fisherman made a dam in the river. And I'm the one who fled later, with nothing in my hands."

Farah still was speaking on the phone. She grimaced and gesticulated and rocked her chair from left to right and right to left. When she finished her conversation, she turned to Sima and said, "Well, what will you do now?"

"I told you last night on the phone. I'm looking for a job. Our savings are running out. Siamak is depressed. I have to find a job, otherwise..."

Farah interrupted her, "I told you that you must be patient. You and Siamak must face reality. This is not your country; you're nobody here. You have to start from the beginning, as we did."

"I know."

"So, what do you expect?"

"Nothing," Sima said. She got up from her chair abruptly, as if a cold wind had blown over her body and carried her away. As she said goodbye to Farah, she noticed again the family photo on Farah's desk and wanted to say, "A Geranium Family," but she didn't.

While waiting for the elevator, she ran into the young Chinese woman who had earlier led her to Farah's office. The woman recognized Sima and asked her, "Did you have a good chat with your friend?'

"Yes, yes," Sima said as she stepped into the elevator with a forced smile on her face and the sweat of humiliation on her back.

"If you want continue to have a relationship with your friend, Farah and her husband," Siamak said, "you'd better forget about me. I couldn't bear her husband even when we were in Iran. Don't you remember how deferential and flattering he was? He always wanted to prove something to me. And now he thinks with his grocery store he is the vice president of the United States. I don't give damn about him."

Sima stepped out onto the street and a warm fall breeze caressed her face. The trees in front of building were filled with colourful leaves, and against the deep blue sky above them, they looked as if they had been painted by a master artist. She breathed deeply and thought, *Siamak is right. I shouldn't expect Farah to perform miracles. I will find a way. I will.*

Line

—∾—

THE LINE SEEMED STRETCHED to eternity, then it vanished in a heavy fog. People of different ages—men and
women, young and old, plus a few children who had
no one at home to take care of them—were in the line. Farid,
a tall man in his early twenties, his deep brown eyes shadowed
with curiosity and anxiety, was looking around, especially at
the people lined up directly in front of him and behind him.
His black T-shirt had a white skull on the front that attracted
the eyes of many. His thoughts wandered; it must be a fantastic
country, he thought, otherwise so many people wouldn't be
lined up in front of this embassy to get a visa—happy those
who would be able to get one and leave. As if he had heard
what Farid was thinking, a middle-aged man ahead of Farid
in the line said, "Young fellow, tell me what kind of dreams
and what kind of fantasies are you spinning about this place?
You should know, there's no such place as the one that you
create in your mind."

This man was about fifty years old, with a salt-and-pepper
receding hairline. He looked smart, with his grey coat, dark
trousers, and a yellow and red striped tie. Well-shaved with a
hint of cologne, he held a half-smoked cigarette between his
fingers. Behind Farid was a chubby woman of average height.
It wasn't possible to say how old she was as her hijab covered
her hair and body. She had exhausted, sad, grey eyes and her
cheeks were dominated by her large nose. The woman also

seemed to have heard Farid's question even though he hadn't uttered the words out loud.

"What does he mean?" Farid asked himself, confused, "Isn't this country real?"

The woman cleared her voice, touched her scarf, an involuntary gesture, and said, "If there's such a place, it's inaccessible. You can't get there, even in your dreams."

A young, tall, thin woman with two big black eyes, and a little girl sucking a lollipop in her arms, asked, "What place are you talking about?"

"The country all of us are waiting to get visa to enter," Farid said. "Have you been to this country?"

The tall woman said, "Have I? Yes, I have. I've been there in my dreams." Those nearby turned to look at her with suspicion.

"It's a wonderful country," she continued. "It is filled with white-skinned people, who have blue eyes and blond hair. In that country, there is freedom. I mean, people are free. When I say free, I mean they're really free. They can wear whatever they like, and they can talk and laugh—yes, laugh, they can laugh. Here, laughter is an offense." With tears in her eyes, she turned her back to Farid and the others who were staring at her.

The middle-aged man in front of Farid said, "All of these are dreams, fantasies. That woman is just dreaming about that country. If such a country really existed, it would be here."

A woman ahead of the man said, "Sir, are you deceiving a child? Me, and many people like me who are here applying for a visa to enter this country, have studied and researched this place. We're not taking a risk. The earth is big. There are many countries on the earth, but we chose this country in particular, because we know it is an ideal place for the young." She looked like a child herself with her colourful scarf and her light brown hair visible on her forehead. Two feverish brown eyes glittered in her shiny, round face.

"But that woman hasn't been to that country yet," the middle-aged man said. "She is simply drawing a fantastic portrait of it, describing it for young people like you, to enthrall you, to mislead you, to drag you to somewhere that does not exist and if it does exist, it's not the kind of place that she is talking about."

"What kind of place is it then?" Farid asked, innocently.

The middle-aged man crushed the butt of a cigarette under his feet, his eyes blankly sweeping over the line of people, and said, "There is no such place. How can I explain...?"

The childlike woman interrupted the man, and said, "What do you mean, there's no such place? Is it possible a country that has an embassy, which is standing right here in front of us, doesn't exist? This country may be inaccessible, but it exists. My son and daughter have been living there for years. They sent me invitation and if I get visa..." She sighed, her eyes saddened, and continued, "This is the third time I have received an invitation from them, but the embassy won't give me visa."

"Why not?" asked Farid.

The woman looked at Farid, her eyes full of frustration. "How do I know? I'm not the ambassador of that country. I don't know why."

The middle-aged man said, "I know why."

"You know everything," the childlike woman snapped at him. "But your words are unacceptable and they follow no logic. Have you ever been there?"

The middle-aged man, proud of himself, paused for a while as if he wanted to measure his effect on others.

Farid told himself, *I'd better not to listen to these people. They are confusing me. I'll have to do some of my own research about this country, read books written about it, and collect information. These people are just expressing their point of view, which is not important, and some of them don't even have an opinion; some can't see even the front of their feet.*

The chubby woman turned toward the middle-aged man and asked, "How did you get a visa? Do you know why they won't give me a visa?"

"There might be many reasons," the middle-aged man said. "I've been there and I have some friends who live there. I know the language of those people. When I was there, I could communicate with them. It's very important that one knows the language of the people."

The man hadn't finished, when another woman in the line interrupted him saying. "Sir, speak for yourself. Over there you can get jobs and you can get information about many things without knowing the language." She was a tall, grave woman with a large body covered from head to toe in a black chador. Her black gloves caught Farid's eyes—strange to be wearing those on such a warm day. "I have been there twice," she added. "But you, sir—obviously you haven't been there at all."

"This gentleman says this place does not exist but then he announces that he knows the language," Farid said loudly, so his voice would reach the woman dressed all in black. "What about you? Have you really been there or are you, too, saying that there is no such land?"

The woman dressed in black said, "For sure I was there. This is the third time I'm going there. The country exists, it really exists. I wish it didn't exist. It is a land of blasphemy and you will lose yourself in this place. Especially the young people—it leads them to hell."

The woman with a child in her arms and Farid spoke at the same time. "What we've heard about this land is completely different. We've heard that over there young people are free to dress as they like, be friends with anyone they want, they can go out dancing and to parties, they can be happy."

The woman dressed in black vehemently shook her hand in the air and waved her arms. "Yes, all that blasphemy: going out with friends, dancing, being happy. Look at our own beloved country: with all its rules and laws, with flogging, imprisonment, and heavy fines, our government still can't prevent debauchery. Boys and girls talk to each other in public, go to restaurants, cinemas, and on dates before marriage. Over there…. Oh, God forbid, it's truly blasphemous—'eyes not to see, and ears not to hear.'"

The childlike woman said, "What's the problem? You call it a blasphemy, but we are young, we want to enjoy our lives."

The woman stared at her as if she were a dreaded insect. Her face filled with hatred and she almost yelled, "You…!" And then, as if she were talking to herself, she continued, "Over there is a real hell."

The chubby woman said, "They say over there it is too cold. And hell isn't cold." And then laughed quietly, as if she had told a funny joke.

Farid ignored the woman's irony and addressed the heavy woman dressed in black, "So, why do you go there then?"

The woman in black straightened her back proudly and with confidence replied, "I have to. My husband is studying theology over there. He got a scholarship from the government and he's been there eight years now. He has asked me to join him. I've been there twice but I can never stay more than a few months. My children go astray there."

Farid turned his back to her and whispered into the chubby woman's ear, "Studying theology in the land of blasphemy!" Both laughed quietly. They could imagine what kind of woman she was and what values she was defending.

The woman with the child in her arms smothered her tears and listened carefully. She started speaking as if she were addressing her own reflection in a mirror, "If they give me a visa, I won't wait for one single hour. I've sold all my properties and traded it for dollars." She lowered her voice so that the woman dressed in black could not hear her, and continued, "I've divorced my husband. He had a Masters degree in law but he still felt he had the right to beat me. I've heard over there is the land of single women. And if they have children, they can get visas easily." She turned to the middle-aged man and asked, "Good Sir, you said you have been there. Can you tell us what you know about over there?"

The woman dressed in black had her back to them, but she had heard what the woman with a child in her arms said. She turned toward her, her arms tightly folded across her chest, and hissed at her crudely, "Yes, that place is exactly for women like you, a divorced, free woman. Over there, you'll be a complete...."

All who heard knew what she meant; she didn't have to finish her sentence out loud. Some looked at the woman in black with disgust, others turned their backs to her and ignored her. The woman with a child in her arms stepped back, her eyes spilling tears. She addressed the woman in black, her voice harsh, "You bitch! Do you really understand what you are talking about?"

"Of course I do. You haven't been there, and you don't know; over there blasphemy is everywhere and it will make a whore of you."

"Madam, you are pessimistic and rude," the childlike woman said angrily. "Your point of view is as black as your clothing. Your imagination about the whole world is black. Over there is the land of freedom, joy, and life. And you say..."

The woman in black turned her back to the childlike woman. Almost whispering, the woman with the child in her arms said to no one in particular, "You see, I am fleeing from these people. The people who always have a rope ready to hang you. I prefer to live in a desert or in a cave and raise my daughter without these kinds of people around her."

The childlike woman said, "But I want to live among people, among people of my age. I want to go somewhere and have many friends. I'd like to dance. Do you remember the day of the soccer game? When we won and the U.S. lost? That day I danced so much, my whole body ached. Yes, I'd like to dance until I die."

Farid smiled and said, "I remember that day. Me too, I danced a lot that day."

The middle-aged man noticed the sapling of love sprouting

between Farid and the childlike woman, and said, "Well, you can dance in your homes. No one has taken your home away from you."

The young woman looked at the man as if he were an idiot and said, "Dancing by myself at home doesn't mean anything. Dancing is something you do with others, something that helps start relationships. It's a way of talking to each other. You can't only talk to yourself. After all, we don't have freedom in our own houses, either."

The chubby woman interrupted her, "So, you want to go there simply to dance?"

The girl's cheeks turned crimson; excited and surprised, she said, "What's the matter with that? Is dancing a sin over there too?"

The woman in black meddled again and screeched, "Obviously, it's a sin. Dancing is a sin. Don't you know that?"

The childlike woman raised her voice too and angrily responded, "No one asked for your opinion. You'd better stay where you are."

The middle-aged man said, "Cut it out. Be quiet please. Do you want them to send us away and waste our day of waiting here for nothing?" He turned to the young girl, advising her. "Don't argue with that woman. And listen to me, over there isn't a place for dancing. If over there exists, it exists for work. And if they give a visa to a young, pretty, intelligent girl like you, and I'm sure they will, they'll give it for your strength and your labour, not for your dancing. Their own people can dance, and they dance very well, so well that all of us, people from this side of ocean, would be astounded and dumbfounded. If you can go there, you'll forget about dancing."

The young girl let the middle-aged man finish and then said, "I won't forget about dancing. I danced even while I was in jail. I was flogged but didn't forget dancing. Do you want me to dance for you right here, in line?"

The woman with a baby in her arms said, "Have you lost your wits or do you want to go to jail again?'

Farid said, "I don't believe you have such courage."

The middle-aged man said, "She is joking. It's good to have a sense of humour. It's good not to forget how to joke in difficult times. But I can't believe you would dare dance."

The young girl started to dance among the people in line, their eyes wide with astonishment. It lasted only a few moments but even the woman in black saw the young girl dancing and her tongue froze in her mouth. The young girl eyed her audience, one by one, as if to say, "Now do you believe me?"

The middle-aged man finally broke the silence. "You *should* leave this country. *Here*, you'll sacrifice your life for your dancing."

"Now, tell me about *there*," the young girl said, pleased with herself. "What kind of place is it?"

The middle-aged man said, "I already told you there is no such place and it doesn't exist."

"Don't listen to this gentleman," Farid whispered to the young girl, "if this country, this place, doesn't exist, then neither do we exist. This line doesn't exist, either." He pointed to the line and said, "Look. These people...."

But there were no people. The line had disappeared into smog, fog, and shadow.

An earlier version of this story appeared in Maple Tree Literary Supplement, *Issue 4, 2008.*

Acknowledgements

—ɯɯ—

I am in debt to Farah Jamali who spent time with me, polishing and editing earlier versions of these short stories. I am also grateful for her positive comments and her encouragement.

I must recognize and thank Lynn Connigham who also edited earlier versions of this work.

In particular, I would like to acknowledge Luciana Ricciutelli, editor-in-chief of Inanna Publications, for her dedication to this manuscript, her keen editing skills, and her commitment to diverse women's writing.

Mehri Yalfani was born in Hamadan, Iran. She graduated from the University of Tehran with a degree in electrical engineering and worked as an engineer for twenty years. She immigrated to Canada in 1987 with her family, and has been writing and publishing ever since. Four novels and two collections of short stories written in Farsi, her mother language, were published in Sweden, the U.S. and Canada. Her novel, *Dancing in a Broken Mirror,* published in Iran, was a finalist for the "Book of the Year" in 2000. She has published several books in English, including *Parastoo: Stories and Poems* (1995): *Two Sisters* (2000); and *Afsaneh's Moon* (2002). A Farsi version of *Afsaneh's Moon* was published in Iran in 2004. A volume of poetry in Farsi, *Rahavard*, was also published in 2004. Her short fiction has appeared in a number of American and Canadian anthologies. She lives and writes in Toronto.